DragonTorch

How Dragons Really Get Their Fire

Robert P. Allen

The Story About How Drake Came To Own The DragonTorch

ISBN-13: 978-1-7356759-1-6

ISBN-10: 7356759-1-6

Cover design by: SusansArt

Printed in the United States of America

Table of Contents

Dedication

Thank you to the two experienced writers who have been so helpful in terms of helping me to bring this book to a reality. Jeannette Windle directed me to many resources that I would never have thought about and how to navigate the waters of publishing independently. Also thanks to Chris Miller who gave me a kick in the pants about how to open the story. Both aided me in ways that can only be called encouragement.

Thanks also to my family who have helped and encouraged in ways that are hard to put a value on. My daughter Rachel who helped me to think through the cover art although her first drafts were not used, they helped me to know what I wanted to convey in the cover art. My In Laws (Roy and Elvia) for their kindly agreement to proof read and edit the book in its almost final version and then for their enthusiasm at the contents.
Sometimes you need someone who cares about you to say those kind words that make you think this might be worth releasing to the general public. Their objective look at my written words helped me to see errors and inconsistencies that I had overlooked. My son was the person who suggested the topic some years ago and the book took its form from his original suggestion. In fact, the idea of a writing a volume two was another comment that I would attribute to him, should there be a request for such a work.

DragonTorch

Prologue

Kate was frantic to get her letter sent to Jan and Drake but afraid that if her dad, or even worse if Mr. Tunis Furbush learned she was writing to someone about her concerns, that would cause problems for her whole family. But the problems could not get any worse than what Kate knew about already. And if help didn't come, and come soon, it could only get worse. There were just minutes to write the note and no time for long explanations, no time for short ones either. She would have to depend on the depth of friendships that she had, even though she'd had no contact with either of them for almost two years.

Kate's handwriting was never as nice as Jan's, but this would do. She quickly reread it and shook her head. No time to write it again, this would just have to do. Quickly she ended the brief letter, but there was one more thing. One more important thing – they must be warned to learn all they could about dragons.

That was it – close it up. Find an envelope. Darn it all, things were never where you expected them to be when you needed them in a hurry. Never one to be stopped easily, Kate quickly made an envelope out of a regular piece of paper. She couldn't even find the tape, so she would have to use glue. Glue was such a mess. She had to get this posted before the mailman left the town for the scheduled weekly postal run. It was not as nice as she hoped but she was out of options. She had a feeling that next week would be too late. The tension in the town had been growing and she should have sent this cry for help months ago.

Kate couldn't recall the postal code for Lamoille, but the name of the town would have to work. She could not really ask around since she knew that just asking would bring suspicion to her plea for help, and she did not want that. Not if it could be avoided. Just before she finally glued the envelope shut, she signed it with her large signature. No one could doubt this was her and no one, especially not Drake or Jan would doubt that she needed help as fast as possible.

Chapter One – Drake

It was a Friday afternoon and not too much was going on. Drake had no idea how quickly that would change. Some people like to believe that Friday is better than any other day, but those are the same people who can't stand their Mondays through Thursdays. Lawrence Alan Drake liked Sundays through Saturdays. That's the way of a cowboy, Drake would tell people. Cowboys are not complainers. Cowboys are not liars. And most of all, cowboys are not quitters! Now don't start thinking that Drake was a typical cowboy with all the cowboy clothes. Sure, he had some jeans that might be considered cowboy clothes. But it isn't the clothes that make a cowboy. It is the rules a person lives by that make them a cowboy. For example, once a cowboy starts something, they are loyal to finish the job. The only small problem with that idea is that in Drake's mind, as he thought about this, was that he had not started anything interesting in a long time. The last time he had been called to help he had spoiled the day for a potential kidnapper – but that's another story. This week, nothing was going on that was nearly as interesting as that. That's how he arrived at Friday, and Drake found himself walking slowly toward Jan's house. He decided to saunter on his way, to see what, or if anything was stirring in the neighborhood. Cowboys were known to saunter, even if that only means to walk slower than a normal walk.

It troubled Drake that he had to walk around to get a look at what was happening around him. He thought that any good cowboy should have a horse but that wasn't going to happen as long as he lived in the city. Although this was a small city, it was still a city. And he certainly wasn't going to complain because, well you remember the cowboy rules. People liked to ask Drake – if you're a cowboy, where's your horse? Drake had a standard response: It takes more than a horse to make a cowboy. He knew he was right about this. Being a cowboy comes from the heart, not from whatever you sit on. He'd already helped a lot of people in his short cowboy career. So much so that it was known throughout the city that if you needed help, you could count on Drake. Drake the Cowboy. So as Drake was prone to do when he walked, he began his walk by picking up a piece of grass and putting it in his teeth like he was cleaning his teeth with the grass. If you know the grass that grew in Drake's town, it didn't really have much of a taste, but he liked the way it looked in the mirrors and windows he glanced at as he passed. He shouldn't be too concerned about what he looked like, but not everyone would get to see a cowboy and Drake felt it was important to make a good impression.

As he walked across his yard and headed up the street, he noticed that Mr. Winters was watering his lawn again. Mr. Winters knew there was a water shortage but there was also a shortage of people who wanted to argue with Mr. Winters about his water usage. The smarter thing to do would be to leave him alone about that. Drake thought about telling him he shouldn't be using water for the lawn but that was not the role of the cowboy either. Cowboys don't tell others how to live unless they are hurting others. I suppose in some way, Mr. Winters was hurting the town by using up water but that is not the kind of injustice Drake was looking to correct. So Drake waved his hand and hollered 'Hello' to Mr. Winters.

Mr. Winters hardly looked up and yelled back. "When are you coming around to mow my lawn?"

"I can come by sometime next week", Drake answered.

"Don't let it go too long".

"I won't. I promise". It was known around town that Drake's promise was as good as anyone's promise. If Drake said he would, people knew he would. Drake knew that keeping your word was a part of being a cowboy too, and he was careful about what he promised to do. But once he promised, you could count on him.

Mr. Winters mumbled something else but by the time he said it, Drake was too far away to hear it. Drake just kept gnawing on his piece of grass and walking. Next to Mr. Winters lived Billy Martin. Billy was a bully and he liked to bother anyone he could. Billy also liked to know that you were afraid of him. He didn't like people he could not make do anything he told them to do. Needless to say, he didn't like Drake. And if Billy wasn't trying to get Drake to fight him, he was making up names that made fun of his name. Silly names, but you know how those can bother people anyway. Billy called Drake names like 'Dork', and 'Drakeula,' and any other stupid thing that sounded like it was close to Drake. Gratefully, Billy wasn't out in the yard looking for someone to bother, so Drake walked on past the house without having to cross paths with Billy. He hurried across the street towards Jan's house. Drake disliked Billy so much that he preferred to cross the street before he got to Billy's house, but today Mr. Winters had distracted him. He made a mental note to avoid Billy's house in the future.

Now it might seem odd to you that Drake knew so many people on his street. He knew a lot of people who didn't live on his street as well. That's the way Drake is. He likes getting to know people. He figures that you can't help people if you don't know them. Granted he hadn't gotten a lot of cowboying work from most of his neighbors, but being friendly was the kind thing to do. He was thinking about all of this as he was walking up to Janet's house. Jan was the person he knew best in the entire town. Drake stepped up to the door and knocked loudly and firmly. He wasn't coming to sell cookies; he was dropping in on a friend.

"Who is it?" A voice came from the back of the house.

"It's me Mrs. Clinton, is Jan home?"

"She's in the back Drake, just walk around."

"Thanks"

Walking around back meant going one of two ways. The long way which went through the gate in the fence and which also happened to be the easy way. Or directly to where Drake knew Jan was, which was in the tree on the other side of the house from the gate. Drake didn't have a preference but today it seemed like he could use the extra excitement of climbing a fence to get into the back-yard. So he walked around to the high fence and began to look for a spot where he could jump up and climb over the six-foot fence.

"Hey, Hey, LA".

Jan was the only person who called Drake LA. Lawrence Alan, for his first two proper names. He preferred Drake but he let just one, maybe two; of his closest friends call him LA. Jan used that just to let him know that he was not sneaking up on her. She saw him before he saw her. Drake looked around for the location of the voice and there she was in the tree again. From her position up high in the tree, she could see most of the street. Drake looked up to see how high in the tree she had climbed today. The higher she climbed, the worse her day. As Drake scanned the tree, he didn't remember her getting this high in this tree or any other tree for that matter.

"How in the world did you get that high up in this tree?"

"I climbed up of course"

"You're going to fall and break every bone in your body and then I'm going to have to feed you with a spoon."

"Don't come up if you're scared."

"I'm not scared; just don't like to see you risk breaking your neck."

"Don't come up if you're scared."

"Be quiet, just give me a minute."

Drake knew that if he started up this tree, he would have to make it as high as Jan because cowboys are not quitters. So he hitched up his jeans as he prepared to climb and he was sure that he heard Jan giggle.

"I can't climb if you're laughing at me"

"Sorry"

Drake started the climb and he was not happy that Jan was so high up in the tree. As he got higher and higher, his knuckles got a little whiter as his grip got tighter and tighter. The closer he got, the more he could hear the small gasps that Jan was making with each small slip or each tree hug that kept him from falling down through the tree. Drake knew that several branches would slow his fall on the way down but the prospect of falling still didn't look to be a fun way to get back to the ground. By the time he got almost as high as Jan, his t-shirt was soaked with sweat from the effort it took to get so high. Lodging himself between two branches, he took a few minutes to catch his breath without spending too much time looking down at the ground.

After a few moments, Drake finally took one long last breath and then looked at Jan. She was sort of smiling because it amused her to watch Drake climb. But beneath the shallow smile there was sadness in her eyes that Drake hadn't seen for a long time.

"What's up?"

Jan lifted up what looked like an old piece of paper that was all crumpled and folded. And suddenly, her face seemed to melt into sadness and tears.

Chapter Two – Opportunity

"Please Help" were the two most obvious words on the paper Jan held, that and a familiar-looking signature that belonged to Drake and Jan's best friend, Kate. Kate had a way of signing her name that outshined everything else that was on the page. She was also the one who introduced Drake and Jan years ago when she used to live in the same house that Billy Martin lived in now. If Kate wasn't so likable, you could be upset that she moved away, but things like that happen when you live with your family. You can't be upset if your best friend's parents had to go somewhere else to find work. But good friends are hard to find, and best friends are impossible to replace. Friends like Kate might move states away, but when you see them again, you pick up right where things left off. You only need to catch up because that kind of friendship never fades with time. Lately, it seemed as though Kate had moved countries away.

The fact is that no one really knew where Kate had moved because Kate's family had moved away almost overnight. She never mentioned it at all that week, and the last Drake or Jan remembered, Kate watched from the back of the family cart as it dragged another second cart behind it. Everyone promised they would write, but no one ever heard where to write to. The two years had slowly passed and every once in a while, especially when they were enjoying ice cream, the two would remember the fun they'd enjoyed with Kate. The reason ice cream made them remember, was because Kate loved ice cream. Most people like ice cream but to her, it was the thing she would promise about, pledge to and even promise to give up if she was lying. Both Jan and Drake hoped that there was lots of ice cream in her new home, but they didn't know because they hadn't heard from her until now.

Drake looked at the letter and then at Jan who had stopped crying and was quietly wiping her face. He decided to take a look and try to understand what the letter was all about. Kate's writing was not always easy to read so he set his mind to figure out what was going on. He started to read the letter out loud in the hopes of making more sense of it than his first glance offered.

Drake began to read slowly. "Please Help. We are in trouble. Please come or my family might not live. Our mouse . . ?"

"Our house!" Jan said.

"Our HOUSE" Drake emphasized but Kate's writing wasn't always clear, especially when she wrote quickly. This letter was obviously written quickly. "Our house is opposite Grave Mountain and between here and Nowhere. Learn all you can about dragons before coming. Time to cowboy up. Please hurry. Kate."

"Dragons? What do you think she means with that? 'Learn all you can about dragons'? "

"You know Kate better than I do, you knew her before I did."

"Yeah, but you and her were together all the time after you met. You were inseparable. She's the one who told me that I needed to live by a set of values. She was the one who told me to live by the values of a cowboy."

"She didn't tell you to do that, she saw that in you. She could see things in people and point them in the direction they needed to go. She knew you needed to live the cowboy way, so she helped you figure that out. That's what she did. Or does." Jan corrected herself. "She's still alive, I'm sure of that, LA."

Drake stated the question that had his mind stirring. "What do you think she means with that? 'Learn all you can about dragons'? Dragons aren't real. Never have been."

"The idea about dragons had to come from somewhere. Maybe it wasn't just from someone's imagination, maybe it was from someone's memory." Jan didn't like to come to definite decisions too quickly and was prone to think of other considerations. It was one of the things Drake liked so much about her.

"Maybe the legend of dragons is a mix of the two different things if there is any reality to dragons at all. You know like two stories that got mixed up and from the two different stories, it was combined to be the legend of the dragons." Drake's statement made half his brain wondering and the other half questioning. The third half of his brain was wondering if they could even find anything close to true about dragons. They weren't even sure where Kate lived. But one thing at a time, and Drake didn't want to get that cart too far ahead of the horse he still didn't have.

"Where does a person find out anything about dragons?"

"I would guess", said Jan, "in the library. There has to be a book about them. Follow me; I know just where to go."

And Jan began to climb down from the top of tree, happy that maybe there was something she could do for Kate. Drake just stared as he watched her climb quickly down, hoping he could learn something about the safest way down by watching her. When Jan was almost to the ground, she looked back up. Drake pretended to be reading the letter again, but he was really studying her path of descent.

"Hey, are you coming?"

"I'm coming, I'm coming." So Drake slowly folded the note and put it in his pocket, trying not to think about what it might feel like if he were to fall to the ground from this high up. Drake didn't mind many things, but things that swayed in the wind made his insides start to move around and once your stomach begins to move quicker than the rest of your body, it rarely ends well. And just as he began to think about the wind, Drake noticed that the wind was beginning to pick up.

Jan started walking towards the library knowing that once Drake got to the ground, he would catch up. She heard some large branches break and then fall heavily to the ground after she had walked a little distance from the tree, but thought it kindest not to turn around and ask Drake if he was okay. In fact, she didn't need to. She heard his typical answer shortly after she heard the deep thud of something hitting the ground very hard.

"It's ALL-right. I'm OK."

Jan answered back without turning: "Didn't doubt it for a second! Now catch up if you can and let's get to the library."

Chapter Three – Library Studies

Finding the library wasn't all that difficult. Libraries don't change locations and in each town, there isn't usually more than one, unless you live in a big town. Just so you know, Drake and Jan did not live in a large town. It was about a ten to fifteen minute walk and during the walk, they both remembered things about Kate that were fun and nice. She was a little pushy but neither one of them talked about that right now. They remembered things like when she broke her arm and colored in the cast to look like the picture of the boardwalk at the beach. You could see things that were very small and very large. Every day she would add to the cast and when she was told it was time to have the cast removed, she actually asked to keep it for another week. Her Mom said that wasn't possible so when they removed it, Kate kept that cast and put it up on her shelf like it was a piece of art. It was art; it's just that the canvas she used was a little strange.

Kate looked at things differently than others, which wasn't all bad, but it did catch you off guard. When you were looking one direction, she swept in from another only because she loved to surprise others. Like the time she learned to ride her bike while sitting on the handlebars, driving the wrong direction. Oh, did I mention that was how she broke her arm, too? But watching her coming up the street, facing backward but pedaling to go forwards, it took you off guard. She also liked to hang from things such as trees, gutters, and beams in her garage. She would hang up there for such a long time you might forget she was hanging around and begin to say things not knowing she was there. Maybe she just liked listening in on other people's conversations. In fact, Kate did get in trouble a couple of times for listening in when she shouldn't have been.

By the time Drake and Jan reached the library, they were both smiling and laughing about their adventures with Kate, but neither of them could remember her ever saying anything about where she was moving to. They would have to figure that out if they were going to find her and help her. But for now, they needed to find something about dragons. They stepped into the library only to be stopped at the door by Mrs. Harcase. She must have seen them coming down the street.

"If you two think you're coming in here to talk and make noise, just find somewhere else!"

Drake wanted to say something back but remembered he had a code he lived by so he didn't say anything mean or rude.

"Actually we're here for research," Jan replied.

Mrs. Harcase actually smiled but it didn't look like it was an easy thing to do for her chiseled face. This must be how the phrase came to be known, to crack a smile, but gratefully her face didn't really crack. "This is nice – what can I help you find?"

"We need to find out all we can about dragons."

Her smile eased back to where her face was more comfortable and she let out a slight "Hmm". "I know where those books normally are but good luck finding one."

"Where are they usually?" asked Drake.

"Well, in our library, your library, dragons fall under several categories. The book of Job from the Bible wrote about dragons, so that might be under religious literature, which is section 200."

"Where is that?" asked Drake.

"She's not done yet LA"

"Then there are dragons in some Greek books, which would be section 900. "

"Then there are books from the Middle Ages that write about dragons, which is also in the 900 Section. And of course, there are dragons in literature, and literature is in Section 800."

Drake was getting impatient and Jan was just looking around. Finally, Drake held up a little finger like he wanted to ask a question. When she took a short breath, he asked quickly "Where is the oldest section about dragons?"

"Doesn't matter really because all the books the library has about dragons have been checked out."

"CHECKED OUT? By who?" both Jan and Drake asked.

"By whom" – Mrs. Harcase corrected. They both shook their heads from side to side, as if to say 'not now'.

"By Billy Martin, he keeps all the books about dragons. I would say he's your local dragon expert in our town. He's the only dragon expert in our town."

Jan and Drake turned and began to whisper to each other. As they did this, Mrs. Harcase noticed someone standing at the counter needing help and she walked away without knowing that she was being excluded from their conversation.

"Anybody but Billy Martin, I try my best to avoid him."

"Everyone does, but we might need him for this."

"I hope not – what rotten luck. The only kid I don't get along with may have something I need to have. Maybe Mrs. Harcase knows something about Grave Mountain."

"That's a good idea, let's ask."

Jan and Drake walked up to the counter and waited for Mrs. Harcase to finish dealing with a stack of late return fees. She didn't get any money from the person but shook her finger at him and told him that if he continued to keep books longer than he should, he might get his name in her book. Obviously, you do not want your name in her book.

"Looks like we'll have to go talk to Billy Martin about any dragon books we need, but we have one more question."

"What else can I help you with?" Neither Jan nor Drake was sure if she was smiling, but there was something in her eyes that said she was happy about them needing help.

"Do you know where Grave Mountain is?"

Do you know how a room goes suddenly silent just as you are about to accidentally burp out loud? Then it feels like everyone in the room is looking right at you. The words "Grave Mountain" seemed to attract every set of ears and eyes in the library. It got so quiet that Drake thought he heard Mrs. Harcase's face squeak a little as the corners of her mouth got very, very tight.

"Why do you want to know that?" Everyone's head was still completely focused on the two who had asked the question.

Drake's heart beat a little faster and he knew this was a cowboy moment. This moment came because sometimes you have to walk the thin line between telling somebody everything you know and telling them just enough and still avoid telling a lie.

"We were going to write a letter to a friend, and we wondered how it would get there," Drake replied. All the heads in the library turned back around and they begin reading what they were reading and watching what they were watching and writing what they were writing. As Drake watched this happen, he wondered what they might be getting into.

Mrs. Harcase lowered her voice and began to whisper. Few things are harder to hear than an experienced whisperer and there are few more experienced whisperers than a librarian. Maybe a person who disarms bombs might be better, but I can't think of any others.

"Grave Mountain is one of those places you can't get to from here. You have to go somewhere else before you can travel there."

Drake grabbed a piece of paper from the countertop and flipped it over. Then he grabbed the pen from the counter and handed it to Mrs. Harcase. She kept right on talking and drawing until the paper was full of arrows and lines. Some lines were rivers and some arrows were mountains and most of the circles were lakes. By the time she stopped talking, Drake felt like he knew more about how to get there but not enough.

He took the paper and headed to the door as Jan followed as close as she could behind him. She knew that Drake had determined he was going to find out what he could, and he would help Kate no matter what the cost. Drake had made a cowboy's promise, even if he hadn't said it out loud.

The last words he heard from Mrs. Harcase as the door closed behind him was, "If you are going to talk to Billy

Martin, tell him three of those books were due last week."

Chapter Four – Billy

As Drake and Jan walked back from the library, they began to talk about how they were going to get those books about dragons from Billy Martin. No matter which way they thought about this in their minds, it didn't look like they could avoid telling Billy why they needed the books, unless they didn't tell him the truth. Drake informed Jan that lying was not an option because cowboys are not liars. Jan even tried to convince Drake to let her do all the talking, but for Drake, being a part of a lie didn't sit comfortably with him either. Nope, if Billy asked, they would have to tell him; maybe they could avoid telling Billy everything that Kate had written. It wasn't going to be easy and most of all, it wasn't going to fun. Nothing with Billy was truly fun.

By the time they got to Billy's house, they had agreed just how much to tell Billy and what they needed the books for. They were going to say they were doing some research for a friend who lived far away. She had asked them to get to understand what they could about dragons, so Jan and Drake were going to put together a short report about dragons for her. They had been told that Billy was the expert and they thought maybe they could ask him a few questions. On the surface, this sounded like a workable plan. As long as Billy didn't get too nosey, but the chances of that happening were slim to none. Billy had a natural tendency of being able to tell when someone was trying to keep a secret.

"Who is it?" Billy shouted after Drake stepped to the door and knocked, softly at first but this last time, it was pretty loud.

"It's Drake and Jan."

"Dork and Jan? What do you want?" Billy didn't usually make fun of the girl's name, especially if they were even the littlest bit cute.

"Billy – we need your help," Drake answered, yelling through the screen door to the back of the house. Billy still didn't make any effort to get up and come talk to them.

"Dork – did you finally decide to face up to a real fight?" Now Billy was coming towards the door in loud, deliberate steps. He wasn't really a small kid, but he was making himself sound a lot bigger and stronger than normal. "Because I'm always ready to teach you a lesson about who's the meanest kid on this block."

"No Billy, really. We need your help to learn more about dragons."

Drake said this just as Billy was about to swing open the screen door, which would have smacked Drake and possibly Jan right in the nose. But at the word 'dragons', Billy froze mid-step.

"Dragons? Who told you I knew about dragons?"

"Mrs. Harcase at the library said that you had read every book there is in the library about dragons. When we were there, she said if we wanted to know anything about dragons that you were the expert in this town."

Billy stared a little into the air, didn't say anything for a moment and then slowly said, "Hmm, no one has ever called me an expert on anything before."

Drake thought he was getting somewhere. "She said you had every book of any value on dragons checked out and that you are always trying to learn more and more about dragons."

"Well, she's right about that. I am always trying to learn more about dragons. Did you know that our word for 'worm' is an old word that originally was the word for dragons?"

So for the next 30 minutes, Billy stepped outside as they sat on the porch and talked without hardly taking a breath about the history of dragons, where they were from and even why they had disappeared. In fact, Billy mentioned, some don't believe they are all gone but just have stayed out of view for the last 500 years. When Billy slowed down his talk about dragons, he turned to the question they both knew he would get to eventually.

"Why do you want to know about dragons?"

Jan began. "We are looking into some research for a friend who lives in a town that doesn't have a library. She asked us to help her collect some information about dragons, so we thought we would put together a short report about dragons for her. "

Billy didn't say much for a moment. He didn't have many friends and talking to people sure seemed easier than beating them up. "Maybe I should write the report for her since I'm the expert on dragons. I don't want you guys to mess it up by making stuff up."

Drake saw where this was heading. "That's okay. We don't want to bother you any more than we already have. We can do this."

Billy, seeing the opportunity to perhaps meet someone who liked dragons and maybe even expand his list of friends beyond zero, thought maybe this would be a good thing. "What's this person's name?"

Jan wanted to make up a name, but Drake saw she was about to lie so he blurted out, "Her name's Kate".

"Kate? The girl who used to live in this house, Kate? I don't remember hearing that she liked dragons."

"Yeah, well things change," Drake said, not wanting to discuss this.

Billy sensed Drake's tone in his voice. He began to focus on Kate. "That doesn't make any sense, its summertime and no one writes reports during summer break."

Drake knew that Billy had a remarkable ability to be able to tell when people didn't want to talk about something and just as soon as Billy sensed that, he would ask even more questions. Drake knew what was about to happen, so he pleaded with Billy. "Just tell us all you know about dragons!"

"You don't have enough time to hear all I know about dragons. You have a plan don't you Drakeula?"

So it happened that Drake was cornered into telling Billy all about the letter from Kate and letting him know what his plan was. He was going to find Kate and help her and her family. Jan hadn't agreed to all this, but it looked like an adventure was planning itself around these three. The problem with adventures was that adventures are uncomfortable. Not that being uncomfortable would slow down a cowboy, but this adventure looked worse than other adventures Drake had been on. If you laid out all the points he knew and all the points he didn't know, the 'didn'ts' were a lot more than the 'dids'. They didn't know where to go. They didn't know how to get there. They didn't know what they were going to do when they got there. About the only thing they did know is that Billy wasn't going to give them enough information about dragons to let them go without him. They also knew they didn't want to bring Billy along, but it was getting clearer and clearer that they didn't have a choice. Drake was sure that he would regret it, but Billy made Drake promise he would take Billy along. Even though Billy didn't like Drake,

Billy knew that if Drake gave his word, he would stick to it. Billy would later admit that he liked that about Drake, but right now no one was saying anything nice about anyone else.

"Let's meet back here at your house tomorrow after lunch Billy. We need to go over some rules before we get started or we'll never make it there."

Billy didn't care much for rules but maybe this was a good idea. He agreed and before Drake and Jan walked away, Drake turned and reminded Billy what Mrs. Harcase had said. "The librarian asked me to tell you that you have to return some books to the library. They're overdue."

"I can't return those books. Those are the ones that will be the most helpful! We're going to need those books. I'll take care of that when we get back."

Chapter Five – Rules

When all three met the next day each one brought things that they believed necessary for the adventure. They traveled to Billy's front yard with their bikes, but that seemed strange. They hadn't really figured out where they were supposed to go. The really odd thing was, each one, without talking to anyone else, walked their bike to the meeting. It was a slow and quiet walk like a person takes when they know they are walking to the principal's office. As they slowly gathered, Billy was the last one to come out of his house. The people who have the least amount of distance to travel are always the last one to the meetings. As they sat under the tree, Drake was the first to speak after hellos and grunts had been said all around.

"Billy, Jan – we need to make sure we are all following the same rules or we just can't get started."

Billy moaned as if he was in pain and Jan gave him a look, turned and continued to listen to Drake.

Drake continued. "We stay together at all times, no wandering. We can't lose anyone on this trip. That means we move forward together, we retreat together and we stay in one place together."

"I don't retreat, Duffus."

"I don't like to retreat either Billy, but if we have to retreat, we all retreat together. That's a rule nobody breaks. If you can't agree to that, we don't go. And if we don't go, we won't get to the bottom of why we need your knowledge about dragons." Drake was trying really hard not to get upset at Billy without letting him get away with behaving poorly. It is odd how some people can push you right to the edge of biting your tongue.

"Jan, what did you tell your Mom?"

"I said we were going on a long bike trip and not to expect us back for a few days."

"Perfect; And you, Billy?"

"No one really cares if I'm here or not."

"Did you mention you were leaving to anyone?"

"What for?"

"Would you mind leaving a note for someone in case they come looking for you?"

"Whatever, I'll be right back" snapped Billy.

Slowly, Jan and Drake were beginning to understand more and more about Billy and why he was who he was. Drake thought again about the fact that there is a story behind everyone's life. We think we know about who they are, then we learn why they are the way they are.

Drake turned to Jan – "That wasn't too much to ask. Do you think that was too much to ask?"

"Billy may not be who we thought he was – make sure you give him a chance before you go too hard on him," Jan said while they waited for Billy to get back. "Which way do you think we're heading?'

Drake began to pull out the map that Mrs. Harcase had drawn, and as he did, he noticed that on the opposite side of the map was a list of names. He got distracted reading the names on the list because one name stood out. Drake happened to notice the name Billy Martin several times on the list. He began to count the times. Billy's name was on that list 8 times.

"What is this?"

As Drake read down the list, Jan had moved over closer to read over his shoulder.

"LA, you are in trouble now."

"Why?"

"This is Mrs. Harcase's list of students with overdue books. How did you get that?"

"She drew my map to Grave Mountain on the back of her list."

Billy walked up. "Let me see that list." And he grabbed the list out of Drake's hand in one quick jerk, except Drake's hand wasn't ready to let go of it. The list was torn in two quicker than anyone could stop it. When Billy saw his name on several of the lines, he tore up what was left of the map.

"Billy that was our only map to Grave Mountain. We needed that to get there and to get home."

"Pretty lousy map if you ask me." Billy groused.

Fortunately, Jan had tape in the things she had packed, and they taped the map back together as well as possible. It wasn't good as new but it was good enough. Drake explained it all to Billy and Billy figured he knew the direction to start. Drake knew that too but since Billy was right, no sense stealing the small victory from him about where to begin. There was sure to be some other times when Drake would have to make a decision not to follow Billy.

As they all got on their bikes and headed out of town, both Drake and Jan looked back at their houses and wondered how long they would be gone. Billy didn't look back at all, but was the first one to the edge of town and never even stopped to think about where he was going. His only thought was that he knew there was going to be some hills to bike up and the quicker they got to the hills, the quicker they could coast down the other side.

Just a little ways out of town, the roads began to change. At first, it was small things like the curb was no longer there. Curbs weren't really missed if you were just riding your bike, but then Drake noticed the gradual changes. After a few miles, there wasn't even room for two carts to pass going each direction. And it seemed like there were fewer and fewer carts going by. After even some more time, the road got a little dirtier and a few more holes. As the day progressed, dirt gradually replaced the hardened clay until it got harder and harder to see any road at all. At a certain point, Drake didn't see any signs of town at all. Funny how things disappear and all of a sudden you notice them and you can't stop noticing them. Of course, there were no more street lights. This is when Drake realized that they would have to find a place to spend the night pretty soon. He whistled to Billy to let him know the plan.

While everyone was biking, there had been very little talking. It's not easy to talk and ride your bike at the same time. You have to save your breath for pumping the bike peddles and not for chatter. Drake had hoped to ask Billy some questions about dragons, but Billy was pretty far ahead of both Drake and Jan and shouting was out the question. Drake could have caught up with Billy but didn't want the two of them to get too far ahead of Jan, so he stayed back. So far Billy hadn't really made much of an effort to stay together. Drake would have to mention that to him tonight. Billy finally stopped when he heard Drake's whistle and waited as Jan and Drake caught up with him.

"Billy, we need to find a place to spend the night. Someplace that's covered."

"There's a large fort up ahead that I built last summer - how about that?"

"You've been up here before?"

"Of course, who hasn't?" Billy looked at Drake – "You haven't been here before?"

"Nope I've never headed out of town this direction."

"I guess you are lucky I could come along. Follow me; it's not too much further."

But it was a whole lot further. Further, than Billy remembered and much further than Drake or Jan were in the mood to go. But since cowboys don't complain, Drake didn't. But Jan didn't have any such code, so she did her share. Didn't bother Billy at all though because he was the leader for the time, and this was as much fun as he had all summer. He stopped a couple of times to get his bearing as the light slowly turned darker and finally into full darkness. If it wasn't for the full moon, there would be no way to see. The clouds were not helpful as Billy searched the land for his hidden fort.

"Ha – there it is. She's still standing!" Billy looked over the fort with a certain degree of pride and amazement. Drake and Jan looked with amazement too, but it was not the same kind of amazement as Billy.

"That's not really standing."

"It's just like I left it. She's a beauty, I'll bet there's still some of the things I left behind in there."

"What kind of things?" Drake asked as he searched his backpack for his flashlight.

"Should be a blanket, some water bottles, and I think I left a rocket launcher here with a few good rocks. Those kinds of things."

As soon as Drake turned on his flashlight, he saw that those things were there, but they were all covered by a couple of months' worth of dust and grime. Only the rocket launcher looked like anything you would want to use right away; however, one of the water bottles looked like it was still good to drink from. Drake recommended that no one do that until they could look at it in the light of day and they all had their own water anyway. The blanket looked like it was unusable after shaking the dust from it downwind; it served as a fairly good ground covering. So much so that Jan decided she would be taking it with them when they left in the morning. There was enough wood around for a fire, but it wasn't cold enough to need one. All of them pulled out their first meal which ranged from a small sandwich to a can of cold soup. Billy and Drake had both brought some canned goods, but only Jan had brought a can opener. She didn't have any cans but thought that maybe someone might. Billy was so hungry that even cold, canned soup tasted pretty good. Drake had a combination of small, packaged fruit bars and some jerky. Who doesn't like beef jerky? It was one of the best parts that made being a cowboy more fun.

"So Billy, when were you thinking about telling us you had a fort out this way?"

"You never asked until just a little while ago."

"Do you have another one a little further on?"

"Nope"

"Have you ever been to Grave Mountain?"

"No, but I have heard of it – and you never asked."

Drake wasn't afraid to ask questions. "How far do you think it is?"

"No idea."

"Well, we better get some sleep," Drake said to nobody in particular, but to everybody in general. But as soon as he said it, he listened for an answer and he could already hear the heavy breathing of both Jan and Billy who were asleep inside the remains of Billy's fort. It had been a long day.

Drake tried to think through the next part of the plan, but nothing seemed very clear. He was coming to the decision that he would have to make it up as things moved forward, but before he actually admitted that to himself, he had drifted off to sleep as well.

Chapter Six – First Casualty

Drake liked to get up with the sunrise, but when he's tired, that doesn't always happen. Today he woke up to the sounds of Jan putting things away into her backpack as he slowly rubbed the sleep away from his eyes. Rolling over, he felt a sharp pain in his leg and realized that he had spent the night sleeping on a small rock that left a large ache in his leg. He made a mental note to clear out any rocks from under his sleeping bag the next time he slept on the ground.

Rubbing some life back into his leg, he asked Jan, "Where's Billy?"

"He said he had a favorite hill around here that he wanted to visit. You were still asleep so I didn't think it would slow us down. He took off about 45 minutes ago on his bike."

Drake rummaged around in his backpack for something to eat and noticed that Billy had left some of his wrappings on the ground.

"We can't be leaving stuff behind like that" pointing to Billy's wrapping and garbage.

"We won't."

Drake stood up to look at the fort that Billy had made and found that it looked worse in the daylight than it did by night. All around it were left-overs from Billy's visits, and various things that he had collected to build the fort. There was a small wooden board that looked like it had been pulled out of the garbage. There were large inner tubes that were all flat. There was also an air mattress that was flat and ripped in several places. It was hard to imagine anyone was proud of this, but Drake knew by what Billy had said, that Billy was very proud of this fort.

All of a sudden, Drake looked up and saw someone walking toward them.

"Jan, someone's coming."

Jan turned and stared, "That's Billy and he's walking his bike."

"And it looks like he's hurt."

Not only was Billy hurt, but his knee was gashed and his bike had taken a serious beating. With his pant leg torn and some marks of blood showing, neither Jan nor Drake could imagine what had happened. They walked towards Billy, grabbing all their things as they headed back to the road that had brought them here the night before. The closer they got to Billy, the worse he looked. His face didn't have the same meanness it usually had.

"Billy, what happened?"

 "I have a favorite hill that I like to ride down out here. I call it Dead Man's Hill, but I didn't think of it as very dangerous until today. It's one of the main reasons I like to come out here. You ride your bike from the backside of the hill, riding as fast as you dare, and then you cross over the top and go down. You pick up some serious speed and every time I've done this before I have never lost control, well until today. Just as I reached the top of the hill, at the worst possible time, my chain fell off and I lost control of the bike. I tumbled all the way down the hill, and I am pretty sure there is a rock stuck in my knee."

Drake started to get angry and Jan stepped in front of him.

"Let me see your knee." Jan seemed to take over. That's how a team works; some people step forward and lead at just the right moment. This was the moment Drake's team needed Jan to take the lead.

Billy slowly pulled up what was left of his pants so that the other two could now see what had happened to Billy's knee. Billy was right. There was a small, sharp rock lodged in Billy's knee, but it wasn't too deep. Billy didn't want to look, but his eyes were drawn to the injury as if it were happening to someone else.

"Just leave me here and I'll find my way home."

"That doesn't happen. We move forward together, we retreat together and we stay in one place together." Drake was very firm about this rule.

Jan was looking at Billy's knee when she said, "I don't think we can do anything but pull out that rock. I think it will bleed more but hurt less. What do you want to do Drake?"

"Can you ride home like this Billy?"

Billy thought for a moment and you could see his face change as he decided what he was going to do. "I'm not going home; I'm going on with you two."

"Your bike is a total loss, this isn't going to work."

"I'll fix it – you can't send me back now. You wouldn't have gotten this far without my help."

"Jan, do you have anything to bandage Billy's knee with?"

"I can find something."

"Go get what you have, we'll pull the rock out of his knee and decide how to patch it up."

Jan took off to see what she had packed that could help. As soon as she left, Drake wanted to start asking Billy some questions, but he remembered what Jan had told him. 'Make sure you give him a chance before you go too hard on him'. Drake knew Jan was right, so he didn't say anything. It was Billy who started talking first.

"Sorry, I shouldn't have risked getting hurt."

Drake wondered how long it had been since Billy had apologized for anything. He didn't sound like he enjoyed saying those words. "It'll work out – things always seem to have a way of getting figured out."

"I really hope you're right."

"I know I'm right. Besides, I'm not ready to even think about quitting yet. You're too hurt to head back home alone and we still have some work to do to figure out what's happening to Kate."

"Why do you think she needs us to know about dragons?"

"I don't know, but I know Kate and that's enough for me. Why did you want to come along? You've never met Kate?" But before Billy could answer, Jan walked back with her hands full and a renewed idea of how to solve this problem.

"Okay, I found some things that are going to help but I don't have everything we need. First thing is to get that rock out. I can't imagine this is going to feel very good."

"Just do it," Billy grunted. He didn't like to look like he was hurting, but he really was. So everyone took their places. Drake decided the best thing he could do was to do the actual pulling of the rock, so Jan helped him wash off his hands and with a clean cloth, he got ready and nodded at Billy. No one said anything but Drake positioned the cloth around the rock and began to count down from 3 to 2, and then 1. On one, Drake pulled the rock out as quickly and smoothly as possible. Even though Billy was in pain, he still found the strength to slug Drake in the shoulder as he screamed when the rock came out. Jan quickly moved in with the bandage she found and wrapped the knee to stop the bleeding. Billy was breathing deeply and quickly through his mouth, and Drake was rubbing his shoulder wondering why Billy had hit him so hard. Billy looked over at Drake, nodded his head a little to the right and raised his eyebrows as if to say 'sorry' for the second time in ten minutes. It was then that Drake knew he wasn't hit because Billy was mad at him. Billy hit Drake because taking out the rock had hurt a lot, and his instincts were to hit someone when things hurt. But it went against Billy's instincts to apologize, and that was a change for the good.

As Jan was wrapping Billy's knee and Billy had his eyes closed in pain, everything seemed to slow almost to a stop. Then a new voice broke the silence that hung between Billy's painful moaning.

"That's a pretty nasty cut there kid. Got any antiseptic to put on it?"

Chapter Seven – Adventure Continues

Have you ever been concentrating on one thing so hard, and then a person comes up from behind and calmly says something you don't expect? Well, that kind of thing can really make you jump. Drake and Jan both jumped. They pretty nearly jumped out of their skin; at least it felt that way. Billy was in so much pain that he just opened one eye, looked at the stranger and then closed it again. He was too busy dealing with his pain to pay much attention to this newcomer. No one realized how important this newcomer would soon become on their adventure.

When Drake had recaptured his breath, he was the first to speak.

"Where did you come from?"

"I was walking down the road with my cart when I heard a scream. I walked over to find out who was here and to see if could help. You all seemed to be doing everything just fine without me, until I saw that you didn't have anything to kill any infection in the wound."

Billy opened both eyes wide at the word "infection".

"Do you have anything that might help?"

"Maybe I do – let me take a look. I'll be right back." The man ran back to his cart to see what he had.

No one had any idea where he had come from or who he was, but it seemed like he had come along at just the right time. Normally, you don't want to trust a stranger, but when you need help and someone comes along that looks like they can help, well in case you didn't know, that's how adventures seem to go. These are the kinds of things that make them adventures.

Drake and Jan were whispering among themselves while the stranger was searching in his cart. Once again they didn't hear him walk back up to their group of three. He could have frightened them again when he spoke, but they were a little more prepared to hear his voice this time than they were before.

"Yep, I found something that should help. Remove the bandages and pour this directly on the open wound. It will hurt and it should foam up a little, but it will help make sure we don't have anything more serious happen, like an infection."

Jan poured just a little bit on the sheared skin and then stopped. But the stranger kept rolling his hands in a circle as if to say, pour more. Billy's eyes were wide open now until finally, the stranger motioned that was enough and took the bottle back. Billy's eyes slowly closed. He just didn't want to move except for the big sigh of relief that the disinfectant part was over.

"Your friend is pretty brave"

"His name is Billy"

"Hello, Billy." Billy barely opened his eyes as if to say I'm not so sure I'm glad you happened along. "My name is Pepper McGee. What are your names? What are you kids doing so far from town?"

 "I'm Jan and this is Drake. We're heading off to see a friend." Jan quickly said, to keep Drake from telling the whole story.

 "Where does that friend live? You're heading out of town."

 "Near Grave Mountain." mumbled Billy, even though he was not feeling well, he wanted to be involved in the conversation.

 "You'll never make it to Grave Mountain with that leg! And besides, no one lives on the mountain, most people who live near there live in Nowhere."

 "Nowhere – that's a town near Grave Mountain? Our friend lives near there."

 "That's where I'm heading," said Pepper. "Sounds odd to say you're traveling to Nowhere, but that's where I'm going. I wish the people of Nowhere would change the name of their town, but somebody thought it was funny and the name stuck." "It's about two day's from here."

 "Of course, that's why Kate wrote the word the way she did. Nowhere is the name of a town." Jan was more prone to catch details like that than Drake, but it made sense to him as soon as Jan said it.

"Looks like all this fixing up your friend has worn him out. How about I help you get over the mountain. We can walk him over and lay him in my cart so you can get to your friend's house."

So it was that after a lot of grunting and dragging, they finally got Billy into the back of Pepper's cart. Pepper didn't complain much, but he did mention that Billy was a lot heavier than he looked. In fact, he said this several times until Drake finally admitted it was true. Drake tried not to complain about anything, but helping Billy over to the cart was about as hard as anything he'd had to do so far on this adventure. But cowboys are not complainers. By the time they got to the cart, both Drake and Pepper were breathing deeply and beginning to sweat despite the cold air. Jan had carried everything she could hold and tried to pad the place where they were going to lay Billy. The cart wasn't much of a cart but it had wheels, and a mule. A few things had to be moved around to make the space that Billy needed, but he found a spot even if all he was able to do was moan and groan about his knee.

They covered Billy with blankets and his coat when he finally was safely in the cart. It was Pepper's idea to cover him because the wind was already beginning to blow colder. It seemed like the air was too cold for the summer, but Pepper reminded them that the weather doesn't really care what time of year it is. Weather believes it can snow any time it feels like it. The higher the pass, the more the weather ignored the rules. There were days when Pepper had gone over this same pass in the middle of winter, and the sun seemed hotter than the warmest summer day. And then he remembered when he went over the pass, and he could hardly see through the snow. He had a feeling that today was going to be one of those days when he could hardly see through the snow. Drake was glad that Pepper knew the way both over Grave Mountain and on to Nowhere. He was also glad that the trip didn't have to be canceled to return Billy home. It would have delayed the trip by too much to have to help Billy get home.

The climb up the path through the mountains was not steep but it was steadily up. This would have been too hard to ride with the bikes and Drake grew more and more at peace with the good fortune that Pepper showed up when he did. He knew that adventures have a way of making their own paths. You could plan your path, but it was always something else that guided your steps. Not only was the path too steep to have ridden the bikes, but since they had first begun the climb, the weather was getting meaner and nastier. At first, it was just the cold and wind. If that had been the only thing, that would have made the trip hard enough. But somewhere up the hill, small little flakes of snow began to twirl around and into the cart. Pepper reached back and grabbed a large coat out of his things and turned to the rest of the group and told them to put on everything they had to keep the cold out.

"I got a feeling this is going to get really cold." And those were the last words he spoke to the team for some time, although he never quit encouraging his mule to keep moving forward.

A little while after Pepper told them it was going to get really cold, a strong gust of wind blew against the side of the cart. It was strong enough to slide the entire cart two feet towards the side of the road. Pepper looked back, nodded his head as if to say 'I told ya so' and turned to face the approaching storm. You could hardly see Pepper through his large coat and big furry hat, but watching him shiver in the cold only made Drake and Jan feel colder. They covered up and prepared for the journey over the pass. It seemed like a good time to talk about what they planned to do when they got to Kate's town, to the town called Nowhere.

Chapter Eight – The Pass

The cart ride was bumpy but not too uncomfortable. Drake noticed that the more they got into the snow, the softer the ride but the colder the air. All three of the kids from the original team were covered by all the blankets and sleeping bags they had and still, the wind seemed to find a way to wiggle through and touch them. At times, it seemed like their skin was directly exposed to the cold, and Drake and Jan kept reaching behind them to see if there was an uncovered part. There wasn't. It was just cold, and the wind felt like it was taking a bigger and bigger bite each time it blew.

 Drake thought to talk to Jan about what they would do next, when Billy started to show signs of contributing.

 "I'm really cold in here! Where are we?" Billy asked.

Billy raised the blanket as if to attempt to look, but both Jan and Drake yelled out – "NO!" but it was too late. The wind came in as if it has a mission to chill them all to their cores. Drake saw Pepper glance back and he was covered with snow and ice hanging from his cap and coat. Both Drake and Jan grabbed the blanket and pulled it back down around them all. With their heads all gathered in the same location, they were able to shout loud enough to overcome the howling of the wind.

"We're crossing the pass in a cart with Pepper," Drake yelled.

"Who's Pepper?"

"He came along after you got hurt and helped us get you into his cart."

"How do you know you can trust him?"

Jan said a little softer than Drake, "We didn't have much a choice".

"He knows the way over Grave Mountain and to Nowhere – and we're heading there now in the back of his cart."

"Where's my bike?"

"There wasn't room to bring the bikes. We had to leave them at your fort."

"You shouldn't have left my bike behind. How are we going to get back home?"

"It was the bikes or one of us. There was no other choice. So, Billy, we have some time, tell us what you know about dragons."

Billy looked at Jan and Drake and realized this was his moment. He saw in both of them that they expected his contribution to be important. They admired his knowledge about dragons. People can surprise you when you expect good things, and Billy was no different. He might be mean, but he was human. Seeing in the eyes of

Jan and Drake an expectation of being helpful, Billy began to change into someone who was helpful. If they hadn't all been in such close quarters with each other, everyone would have been more comfortable, but things don't usually happen like you expect them to, especially on adventures. Billy cleared his throat and began to teach them what he knew about dragons.

"Lots of people think dragons aren't real but that is just because they have never seen one. There are a lot of things that are real that many people have never seen. Just because you have never seen something, doesn't mean it can't exist. Stories about dragons go back as far as ancient Greece and China. Both started about the same time in history, and strangely both have some of the same basic traits and stories. Even the word dragon comes from a word meaning water-snake, and before that, the word comes from an old word meaning worm. All the stories center around them living in the earth, and most stories make them out to be loners. They have never been known to live in groups or in family units. There are a few legends about the source of their fire, but not all dragons breathe fire. From what I've read, there are a few different types of dragons."

Drake softly repeated some of this to himself, trying to remember as many of the details as possible.

Billy continued. "I have found stories about dragons that fly, dragons that only live underground, dragons that are known for their digging and some that have a keen sense of smell."

"Keen sense of smell? What would a dragon do with a keen sense of smell?"

"Dragons are known to have a love for gold, and those with a great sense of smell can smell gold through miles of solid rock," Billy answered Jan's question without even the slightest hesitation. "Not all dragons steal gold; most of them find gold for themselves. But they don't like to share their gold after they have laid claim to it. They would rather die in battle than share their gold."

"One trait I found, which also seems to run through time is that dragons never forget a favor. So few people ever show any act of kindness to dragons to learn how loyal they can be. But dragons are very loyal to any act of kindness because acts of kindness are so rare in the life of a dragon."

Jan started to wonder if Billy was talking about dragons or about Billy. But she kept that to herself.

"What if we do run into dragons? How can we defeat them?" asked Drake.

"I don't know that you can defeat them. There are stories of dragons that were defeated but usually, they died of old age. There are a few stories about piercing their thick skin but those are very few. To pierce their skin you need to find a weak spot. Most dragons do not have weak spots.

There are only a few stories about actually defeating a dragon in battle. More often, someone found a dead dragon that had died of old age, and that person would claim that they defeated the dragon. There are no proven recorded stories about any dragon being defeated in battle."

That was bad news to Drake. He was starting to wonder just how dragons were going to fit into this adventure, and what he might have to do if there really are dragons. But Kate's letter came with a warning about dragons.

"Tell me the legends about dragons, maybe we can find something in the stories that might help us."

"I'm not sure they will help, but there are a lot of legends. Do you want them in order of the age of the legend or in order of how many times a legend is mentioned?"

Jan was dosing off about now, but Drake was still focused. "Tell us the stories that are the oldest first."

Billy started speaking again about the legends and stories. He would go on for hours while everyone in the back of the cart was being pushed around by the wind and the weather on the pass. The weather wasn't getting any calmer; in fact, it felt like it was about as bad as weather could get. A couple of times the cart slide sideways and Billy would stop and wait to see what would happen. Through the loud wind, they could hear Pepper telling his mule to keep moving or we would all die up here.

As Billy began to run out of stories and legends, a stronger gust than ever before blew the cart towards the side of the road. Which side neither Billy nor Drake could tell. But they could tell the cart started to slide and then to lean. As the cart was sliding, Jan woke up and was startled by the sideways movement. She screamed as she felt the entire cart begin to slide sideways down the side of the road. Knowing they were on a mountain, there was no way of knowing if they were sliding into the hill or over the edge of the mountain. They heard Pepper's voice above the wind fighting to keep the cart on the path even if the path was completely covered by snow and drifts. It wasn't until the cart stopped sliding that everyone in the cart realized they weren't heading down the side of the mountain, but towards the ditch that ran between the path and the mountain. Drake threw the blankets off of his face and looked up in time to see Pepper looking back at the cart.

"Time for you boys to get out of the cart and earn your keep. We have to get this thing back on the road and find someplace to spend the night. This weather is going to kill us all if we push through the night."

Jan ignored being referred to as a part of "you boys", gathered her coat around her and jumped out with Drake and Billy. Everyone looked at her and just shook their heads. It was too cold to argue.

Pepper did not look good. Covered with snow and ice from the storm he looked more like a snowman than a living human being. As he shook off the snow and un-wrapped his face from the scarfs that protected it from the storm, it became evident that Pepper had been ready for this weather but he still didn't look very happy about it.

"I need everyone to help get this cart back on the road. We have to help my mule get this thing back up on the path. Drake and Billy, you two grab a shovel and dig out any snow that will slow us from getting back up -- but don't dig any dirt. Jan, find some feed for the mule and try to calm it down while we get ready to help push the cart back up on the path."

Everyone moved like they knew what to do, but Billy had never spent any time shoveling snow. Drake had done some, but he always waited until the storms were over to start shoveling. Trying to move snow while the wind was blowing so hard seemed useless until they both realized they had to throw the snow with the wind, not into the wind. As soon as that was realized, things progressed quickly, and they were ready to help the mule pull the cart back on the road.

Pushing the cart back up was not easy and Billy felt his sore knee giving out several times. But he kept his eye on Drake, and as long as Drake wasn't ready to quit, Billy was determined to work just as hard. About the time everyone wondered if they could get the cart to move, it budged an inch, then a foot and in a quick motion, ended up out on the path. Pepper had been at the front of the cart, pulling and guiding his mule which turned out to be a good thing as he smoothly guided the animal to the path instead of off the other side of the mountain.

Everyone was warmer now after working so hard to free the cart, but Pepper instructed them not to remove their coats. Screaming over the wind, Pepper told them it was better to be too warm than get too cold. Everyone climbed back into the cart, Pepper turned and said something that didn't sound very good.

"I know a place we can stay the night, but when we get there I'll do the talking. Old man Francis doesn't like people much, so no matter what; don't complain about whatever I say."

They climbed into the back of the cart and nodded their heads. The heat from the exercise of getting the cart out of the ditch was quickly beginning to disappear. As the cold blew in, no one had much of a desire to question Pepper.

Chapter Nine – Francis

It was less than an hour after pushing the cart out of the ditch that Pepper came to a stop. When Drake and Billy looked up over their blankets, Pepper motioned for them to cover their faces and stay out of sight. He looked at the old house that sat on the side of the hill. It was built into the side of the hill so that it was difficult to tell where the house stopped and the hill began. In fact, it looked like the grass of the hill didn't stop at the roof, but grew over the roof. Windows on the front of the house had been covered up by shutters that hadn't been moved for years. Vines that grew up the side of the walls on the outside had made the window inoperable, but that went along with everything else. There were several signs posted, telling anyone who passed not to bother stopping. It was obvious that people were not welcome here.

Next to the house, there was a small stable-like structure -- as much a lean-to as a stable. Just like the house, it merged into the side of the mountain and went much deeper than the structure appeared. You couldn't tell how far in it went, but there were all kinds of animals gathered inside the shelter. The barn actually looked better kept than the house, something Jan noticed only later. The animals in the shelter were not a normal mix of animals. Animals that don't usually come together peaceably were sitting down and seeking protection from the storm together. It didn't make much sense, but then it was too cold to think too much about it.

Pepper looked around and carefully, slowly read the signs posted. Then he stepped up on the porch very softly. As he stepped onto the porch, Pepper took a deep breath, then turned to be sure that the blankets were covering everyone. He took that final step forward and knocked softly on the door. When no one answered, he knocked again but this time a little louder. Finally, he raised his fist and banged on the door with slow, steady pounds that resounded right over the wind. It sounded like he shook the whole building.

"Go away." Came the gruff reply from behind the old wooden door.

Pepper didn't answer, but continued to pound on the door.

"There is no one home who wants to see who is at my door."

Pepper knocked some more. The more the voice would shout, the louder Pepper's knock would seem to get. Until finally boot steps could just barely be heard crossing the rooms inside. The voice approached the door without stopping his yelling to quit beating on the door. For a moment, the person who belonged to that voice just stood on the other side of the door screaming to stop the beating, and Pepper just continued to beat as loud as possible. Then the door flew open with such speed that it would have scared Pepper had he not been expecting it.

An old man appeared at the door and looked Pepper up from top to bottom. He swiveled around lightly on his feet for someone who seemed as old as he did. Wearing ragged clothes that had seen their share of winters and summers, he was dressed a little lighter than the weather demanded. It was probably because it had been summer weather only recently.

"What do you want?"

"Francis, my mule is cold and needs a place to stay for the night."

"How do you know my name?" The old man got right into the face of Pepper and looked so closely at his features that you might think he had almost lost his reading glasses and was trying to read the smallest of print in the smallest of books.

"I've been here before and I know you are a man who cares about animals."

"I do care about animals – you are right young man. What do you want?"

"I would like to keep my mule in your barn for the night if I can."

"Of course you can, if you know me, you know that I do not refuse any animal shelter, as long as there are no acts of violence against the other animals." Francis gave the mule a look over and said, "I have never had any trouble with mules. You can put him in the barn. I will make sure he gets something to eat while he is there."

"Would you mind if I stayed with him in the barn?"

"You cannot stay in the barn – that barn is for animals. Why would I want a human being stinking up my clean stable? If you enter the barn, you will give the animals something to fear. Stay out of the barn or I will shoot you."

"Well then, do you mind if I sleep in your house while my mule gets some needed rest? I would just take a small space on the floor by the fire."

"Go away. I don't want any guests in my house. Leave your mule in my barn if you wish, but you cannot stay with me."

"If I stay outside, I'm likely to die of cold. I know you don't care about me, but would you have pity on my mule who would be forced to live without a master?"

"I guess I cannot have you dying in the cold. Not sure what a mule would do without a master" – but he smiled a little at the thought of Pepper freezing in the night. Then he seemed to wipe that grin off his face and continued on. "I guess you can come in, but do not make a mess and do not expect anything to eat from me. I do not feed strangers."

"I can bring in food for myself; let me have my servant bring that in."

"Your servant? You did not mention that you have a servant. I suppose you want the servant to sleep on the floor as well?"

"How forgetful I'm getting. I do have a servant. Jan, please bring in enough food for Francis and us. Jan will not be any bother and besides, how shall we share a meal if she doesn't come in to prepare it? Quickly Jan, bring the food in before we all freeze."

"That looks like a lot of food, how much does your servant eat?"

Pepper ignored the question and looked over at the fire. "My, this is as hot as you build your fire in this weather? Jan, tell the wood-boy to bring in some more firewood to heat up the flames so we can cook this food?"

"Wood-boy? What is a wood-boy?"

"A wood-boy is a boy who carries my wood for me. I don't suppose you have a wood-boy?"

Francis just shook his head as a silent 'no'.

"That's alright. Then I guess we'll have to use my wood-boy. What good is a wood-boy if they can't carry in the wood?"

"What good indeed! " Francis affirmed, but a little confused.

Francis watched as Billy walked in, his arms full of wood up to his chin and he laid it all down next to the fireplace. As soon as he set down his heavy load, he began to build the fire to be a fire you could be proud of. Billy wanted a fire more substantial than just a few simmering logs. Within a couple of minutes, the front room was getting very toasty. As everyone was getting comfortable, Pepper slapped himself on the side of the head. Francis quickly turned and stared at Pepper wondering why he would do that.

"I must have lost my mind – since I'm sleeping on the floor, I'll need my bedding. Billy, please have the baggage carrier bring in our blankets." Turning to Francis, "Our guest doesn't want us to dirty up his floor by sleeping directly on it, do you Francis?"

"Uh, of course not. I do not want dirty floors. You have a Baggage Carrier? How many people do you keep with you in that cart?"

"Didn't I mention my baggage carrier – it must be the cold of the storm that has frozen my brain. Of course, I have someone to carry my baggage; what kind of traveler would I be without a baggage carrier? Billy, please tell the baggage carrier to carry in our baggage and get things settled around the fire."

And so Drake was the last to join the group within the shelter and protection that the house offered. He carried in everyone's blankets and sleeping gear. He had to make several trips and because most of it was covered with snow, he shook off the snow to avoid bringing water into Francis's house. The rest was laid out around the fire in an attempt to dry it off before they had to sleep on wet bags and blankets.

It was good to be inside the house. It wasn't that the house was so great, but the protection from the wind was important and the warmth of the fire and hot food brought up the spirits of the entire team. And after a day in the storm and the cold, they all needed some cheering up. Not much was said as it was clearly established that the Old Man didn't like people, because he didn't like talking with people. Not wishing to stretch their welcome any more than they already had, everyone ate in silence and then retired in silence. They were all glad to get some rest.

Chapter Ten – On to Nowhere.

In the morning, it was Drake who was the first to wake up. He looked around, noticed the fire needed to be stoked so he added some more wood. The others seemed restless as the front room had gotten colder because of the lack of heat from the dying fire, but as the heat grew stronger everyone settled in for more rest. Drake decided that he might get things ready for breakfast, so he lined up the food that would be required to feed everyone, including Francis.

 After having done all that he could before everyone was moving, he sat at the table and enjoyed the calm and the comfort of being in an actual house. It hadn't been but two days since he left his home, but the distance traveled made it seem like a longer time. As he looked around the house, he began to notice some of the things that were scattered about. Since Francis didn't like company, he never bothered to prepare for anyone to come into his house. He also wasn't very inclined to clean up to impress anyone since he didn't like visitors.

Laying on the table was an open book of hand-written notes. Drake wasn't comfortable reading someone else's notes, but his attention was drawn to this since there wasn't much else to do. Slowly he turned the book right-side up, looking to be sure that Old Man Francis was not entering the room. Drake noticed that all the notes were about the state of different animals that had passed through the stables of Francis. There were the typical notes you might expect to find about squirrels and birds, but there were also notes about how a mountain lion had come by that had been shot by a hunter. The hunter had only wounded the animal. Francis documented how he healed the big cat. But it was mid-way through the open page that Drake noticed the word "dragon". Drake took such a deep breath that you would have thought that everyone sleeping in the front room would open one or both eyes, alarmed at the noise that broke the morning stillness. Billy was the only one who didn't move. Shortly afterward, everyone but Jan rolled over and dozed back to sleep. Jan knew by the sound of Drake's gasp that something significant had just happened. She began to get up and start moving. She intended to find out what had happened.

When she got to the table, she gave a look at Drake as if to say – what is going on?

"Do you know what Old Man Francis does?"

"From what Pepper told us, he cares for animals."

"It's more than that. He runs an animal hospital of sorts. All kinds of animals know to come here when they are hurt. He heals birds, beavers, dogs, any kind of animals that need help."

"Well, that's kind of nice – I mean someone has to help them."

Drake began to speak slower. "He also heals mountain lions, alligators and dragons."

"Dragons? He told you he heals dragons?"

"It's right here in his book. See, the back page, he listed that he worked on a dragon, but the dragon didn't survive." Drake pointed down on the listing on the page and Jan read it slowly.

Sure enough, the dragon had been at Francis's home for three days and in the three days, while it stayed with Francis, the injury progressed from bad to worse. The dragon had a very bad burn that never seemed to stop burning him deeper and deeper. According to the notes, it was something Francis had called 'Deepest Mountain Flame Burn'. Francis had never seen it before and kept notes about it as good as any professional doctor. He wanted to know how to cure it just in case he ever saw it again. It was only near the end of the dragon's life that he began to stop the destruction of the Flame, but it was too late for the dragon. His notes said that the Deep Mountain Flame Burn continued to destroy even after the heat appeared to have left the wound. The dragon was buried behind the stable on the side of the mountain. Francis noted that it took three days to dig the hole and cover the dragon with a respectable grave. He also had some kind of numbering and letter system that showed how to locate this grave if it was ever needed. Drake noticed that the grave numbering system started much earlier, even from the beginning of the notebook. A lot of animals had been buried on this mountain.

"This is it – we are on Grave Mountain!" Drake said in a very excited voice just as Francis walked into the room.

"Of course it is, you fool! Where did you think you were? Only locals know it as Grave Mountain. I am not even sure what everyone else calls it. " Then Francis muttered something to himself about how much he preferred animals to any human as he looked at Jan with his eyes open and his bushy eyebrows lifted up suspiciously. "Well, aren't you supposed to be the servant? I don't see any food ready to be served. I need to have a talk with your Master. And shouldn't you be picking up all the beds – I'm not sure your Master knows how lazy you two are when he's is not watching over you."

Drake and Jan got up from the table quickly and began doing the things that Francis expected them to be doing. Billy woke up as well and made sure that there was plenty of firewood available if needed. But Pepper remained in bed – which seemed strange. Yesterday was a rough day and he had driven the cart through the storm for the entire day. It wasn't until Francis raised a cup of coffee, and told Drake that he better take a look at his Master cause he's not looking very well. Francis was very sure that he didn't want the guests in the house any longer than they had been, and said before Drake walked over to Pepper that no one was welcome to spend any more time at his house. The storm had ended and it was time for them to get moving.

Pepper was dripping with sweat when Drake walked over to check on how he was. He knew right away that Pepper was sick. He turned to plead with Old Man Francis to let him stay longer, but Drake knew before he asked what the Old Man would say.

"No – you cannot stay – you must leave today, this morning."

Seeing that there was no room for any discussion, they all began to pack up their things and were ready to leave. This time, it was Billy and Drake that carried Pepper out to the cart and laid him in the back where they had laid Billy only the day before. The sun had come out and the snow had begun to melt so the path was clear. All three of them climbed up on the seat of the cart, and Drake took the reins after some help from Francis to get the mule hooked up.

Just before they were about to leave, Jan nudged Drake and pointed to the side of the mountain where there were 1000's of graves! Some very small and some very large. No doubt about it, this was Grave Mountain. Old man Francis stood at the door as if to make sure they really left. Just as Drake was about to snap the reins to get the mule moving, he turned to Francis and asked.

"What do you think it was that killed the dragon?"

"My dragon tongue is not that good. Most dragons speak human tongue, but not very well. He called it 'Deepest Mountain Flame'. I always thought that was just a legend, but he said someone had it and was using it against all the dragons. He said dragons were being made to work by a new Keeper of the Flame, down in the mine. "

"The mine?"

"Yeah, the gold mines, on the other side of Nowhere."

Jan turned to look at Drake who was already turning over this new information in his mind.

Billy watched and listened to all this with his mouth hanging open. He turned to Drake and Jan and mouthed the word silently to them. "Dragons?"

Chapter Eleven – The Outskirts of Nowhere

The sun was shining bright and the ride down into the valley was easy, compared to how things were coming up the other side of Grave Mountain. With the snow melting, more and more of the valley began to open up for the adventurers to see. Drake and Jan filled Billy in on what they had found out about dragons in Old Man Francis' book. Billy seemed to remember something he had read, so he climbed into the back of the cart and dug around for his books. Unfortunately, some of the books looked pretty beat up from having been used to keep the snow from coming into the cart the day before. He was sure that he would be banned from the library for life when he got back home, but for now, he was looking for a particular book where he remembered reading about this legend -- The Legend of the Keeper of the Flame.

Trying hard not to disturb Pepper, Billy finally found the book he was looking for, but he had to move around a lot of stuff to get it up without tearing the pages. The book had been hit by a fair amount of snow, and if you know much about books, you know that books and water don't mix very well. Billy closed his eyes and shuttered as he imagined Mrs. Harcase's face, and the lecture he would receive about the value of books in her library. He opened his eyes, shuttered again, and then climbed over to the front seat to join Drake and Jan.

"Here it is – I knew I brought this one." Billy opened the book and was turning the pages quicker than anyone could read. "Here we are, Uncommon Legends of Dragons." Billy turned as if to narrate through the book for Jan and Drake. "These are legends that are not widely known but have been found in some old songs and stories."

"The Legend of the Keeper of the Flame. No one knows for sure how dragons light their internal flames. Some have believed that when the dragon is old enough, the flame will light by itself. This is hard to verify since no one has ever claimed to be present when the dragon's first flame was lit.

Some believe that the flame of the dragon burns so hot that it cannot be any ordinary flame. Hence it must be a flame that has its source from deep within the earth, perhaps a volcano or something close to the center of the earth.

Some believe that there is a special place where all dragons go that is bred into their unknown traditions, much like the spanning salmon who all know where to go to lay their eggs. If such a place exists, it has never been discovered.

There is a small group of Dragonology experts (the study of dragons), who believe that there is one dragon who is the Keeper of the Flame. He guards this flame with his life, and all dragons must come to him to have their flames lit. This flame is like no other flame. It can reside within the dragon without burning them, but when touched to the scales of the dragon, it never stops burning. The Keeper of the Flame ties all fire-breathing dragons into a community, and has the right to demand service in exchange for the Lighting of their Flame. The Keeper doesn't usually demand anything but gold. The Keeper of the Flame is as close to a King of the dragons as there is, but the dragons won't remain together once they have received their flame. Dragons normally live in solitude, but they will gather to receive their flame. A dragon's desire for the flame is too hard to resist."

Billy took a breath. "So it's real? The Legend of the Keeper of the Flame is real. Dragons are real."

Drake tried to put together some facts that were coming together pretty fast. "Okay, it looks like – maybe – dragons are real. It is also clear that we just crossed over Grave Mountain and it was real as well. Also, it appears that there is a town called Nowhere. We seem to be getting closer to a city, because I'm beginning to see signs that this road has been traveled over. It even sounds like we might know where the gold mines are and how to get to them. I still don't understand how all this puts Kate's family in danger?"

Drake looked at the other two and they just stared back at him. No one knew the answer to that question yet. And while they were all silently thinking about Kate, Pepper started to wake up and ask questions of no one in particular.

"Where am I? What happened to my cart? What day is it?"

Drake began to take charge again. "Jan, can you get Pepper something to eat and drink? It sounds like he's beginning to come around. Billy, is it possible that you can find a pair of binoculars or something like that in any of that stuff? I think I saw something like that yesterday. Take a look in Pepper's stuff too. I'd like to know what kind of town we are going into if possible."

And just as Drake said that he came around a turn in the road and saw a signpost that let him know they were closer than he thought. It wasn't anything official, but it looked like it had been carved from a discarded piece of wood from the side of a house or barn that had burned down years ago.

"Nowhere – 5 miles."

There was still no sign of any town, but the path was beginning to look like a road again and there were fewer and fewer holes to avoid. Still, the road on this side of the mountain never did show signs of being paved. More like cobblestones that had been laid down ages ago when this land was populated by another generation of people. Drake squinted to see something in the distance, but it was Billy who first pointed out the town. Maybe the name of the town was too kind of a word to describe the place they were headed. The reason Drake had not seen it was because all the houses had coverings of moss on the roofs, so that the color of the grass and the color of the roofs were almost the same. If it had not been for the smoke coming from some of the chimneys, it might have been a long time before anyone knew they were coming to a town. Since the day was beginning to get warmer, the only reason for smoke was that in some homes people were cooking something. There was no need for heat in this valley on this day.

Drake still wanted to get a view of the town, so he pointed towards an open meadow and let everyone know they were going to hike up there and take a look. With Pepper having gone back to sleep after eating and drinking some water, they all felt it would be best if they left him in the cart. There was no one approaching from either direction and he would be safe there. They grabbed their backpacks and headed up to get a look at the town. Hills don't look as steep or hard to climb from a distance as they are when you start climbing, so it took a little longer than was expected, but eventually they got to where they overlooked the entire town. There were a lot of people who seemed to be heading away from Grave Mountain, so it made sense to believe that the mine was towards the mountain on the other side of the valley. Since Kate's letter told them she lived between the mine and Nowhere, there appeared to be only a few houses that could be hers. By a process of elimination, they narrowed Kate's house down to one of three that were in that direction -- if they had guessed right about the direction of the mine. Just as they were about to return to the cart and head into town, Jan noticed a cart heading into town from their direction.

"It that Pepper heading into town?"

Drake turned the glasses towards the cart and reported. "Yes – he must have woken up after we were out of range and started heading into town on his own. I hope he's alright."

That was exactly what Pepper was doing; he was driving the cart into town. What no one knew was that Pepper was not happy with them abandoning him in the cart along the path into town. At least he thought he had been left behind. He knew he had been sick, but couldn't have known the team intended to come back and take him to find some help. He was also under the impression that the kids had gone through his stuff, which they had when they were looking for binoculars, and they had taken some of his things. Of course, everything sounds alright when you hear the full story, but at this time Pepper only believed what he thought he knew to be true.

It was Drake that got up first, picked up all his things and shouted, "Come on, we have to catch up with Pepper! He's got most of our stuff." And it was true, they had not been thinking to leave Pepper, so they left sleeping bags and food on the cart. When they all realized this was the situation, Jan and Billy followed Drake's lead and headed after Pepper, down the hills toward the town, in the hope of catching up.

Chapter Twelve – Kate's House

As Drake, Jan and Billy raced down the hill in an attempt to catch up with Pepper, it suddenly occurred to Drake that there was a lot more distance between them and Pepper than he first thought. Running downhill had already caused everyone to run faster than they should be running. Before they knew it, they were all jumping over downed trees and off large rocks. There were a few ditches that were pretty muddy that they jumped over until they got to a shallow but wide creek. Hopping over this creek wasn't the most graceful thing a person ever did, because when you jump over a creek, the other side of the creek isn't always fit to handle someone leaping onto it. When that happens, the creek bank falls away into the running water and your legs start spinning and digging in the hopes of staying out of water. Sometimes your legs don't get wet but this time they did. They were all stopped from their pursuit and hope of catching up to Pepper.

Everyone was slowly climbing out of the water, breathing harder than expected. There was also heaviness to the air that Drake didn't notice until they had begun to run. When jumping over a creek turns into jumping into a creek, it slows you down and takes the excitement out of catching up. And of course, Billy's running was slowed by his sore knee that was still in the process of getting better, since Drake pulled the sharp rock from it just a few days before.

After making sure everyone was okay, Drake looked up and saw that Pepper and his cart were at the edge of the town, and they wouldn't be able to catch up. So they all got cleaned up as much as possible and started a slow descent into the town called Nowhere to find Kate. This time, the walk down was slow and deliberate. Drake was looking left and right, trying to find the easiest path down the side of the hill for Billy. All the time he kept an eye on the buildings they hoped would be where Kate lived. He really wanted to find the quickest path through the town to finally get to see Kate again face to face.

By the time they reached the road, Billy was the first to admit that he was hungry. Jan agreed. They had walked so much that it was time to stop and find something to eat. Unfortunately, they had not thought to be without most of their supplies, or they would have brought their food with them. Only Billy had anything to eat and usually, he wasn't prone to share. Drake was the first to state what he thought everyone knew.

"Billy, you were the only one who was smart enough to bring any food with you."

"Neither of you grabbed anything to eat?" Looking back and forth at Jan and Drake, and they were both nodding their heads saying no.

"Well, let me see what I have. I have a few things that might help." And so Billy once again felt like things would have fallen apart without him, which is something that

Billy didn't usually get to feel. If you know what it is like to have saved an adventure, then you understand how pleased Billy was that he was able to do that. It was the complete opposite of when he hurt his knee, because he thought that he was going to be the reason they all went home without doing what they set out to do.

Billy pulled all kinds of things out of his backpack. In fact, it was surprising that Billy had grabbed so much food before jumping off the cart. Jan believed that he had a lot more to eat in his backpack now than he did two days ago. There were small cakes wrapped in clear wrap, cans of food and snack containers. The cans were of no use since the can opener was sitting in the back of Pepper's cart. But the rest was good, and even Drake admitted that he hadn't realized how hungry he was until they stopped for a quick bite to eat. It turned into several bites, truthfully.

They walked as they ate and found that by the time they finished what they decided they could eat for one meal, they were at the bridge on the very edge of town. The bridge crossed over a deep gully that was normally dry this time of year, but because of the recent storm, had a significant flow of water. There was one road that led into Nowhere from this direction, and that road then went in all directions towards the houses. There wasn't any kind of barrier from this direction, because so few people traveled over the mountain pass that it wasn't worth the work to construct some kind of wall or protection. The homes near the river appeared to be nicer, bigger homes, built with more care. The more they walked into the town, the closer the houses were to each other and the smaller the road became. By the time they got to the very center of the town, the roads were very close to the homes. There were no front yards in Nowhere.

They had arrived on a market day, which meant that the flowers and food were in great abundance. Drake knew that they had to find Pepper among all these merchants if they could. So he told Jan and Billy that it would be best if they split up to find Pepper. They headed off in different directions with a plan to meet back where they began in one hour. They must get their things back! No one had much money, but there was food and their things with Pepper if they could find him.

As Drake walked through the market, it was surprising how many different things he noticed. First of all, there were the smells of the market. The flowers were located at the edge of the market. This was so that after everyone bought their things, they could grab a bunch as they were heading home. No one likes to carry flowers around all day. But after the flowers came the fruits and vegetables. There aren't a lot of vegetables that have an appealing smell, but the fruits were stronger and almost made your mouth water. Knowing that he didn't have enough money to spend on anything he didn't need made the fruit smell the sweeter and more desirable. Still walking towards the center of the market, Drake came to the meat and right next to those, the spices. Almost overwhelming at times, the spices and oils were a distraction to finding what Drake was looking to find.

Since he had spent a full day in the back of Pepper's cart, Drake knew Pepper wasn't carrying food to sell. He would have to find the area where small things were sold, which didn't look like this section of the market. So he kept walking deeper and deeper into the market, towards the center of town. Then something struck him, but he couldn't quite figure out exactly what it was. He looked around in an attempt to put his finger on what it was. From face to face, Drake looked without finding who or what he was seeking. It got to the point that he stopped and took the time to seek the eyes of every person within view, and he was confirming in his mind what he already sensed with his heart. There was something seriously wrong with the people of Nowhere. Drake just didn't know what it was, but he knew something was very wrong. He could not put a name to the problem, but it was as real as the people in Nowhere.

As Drake stood in the center of this crossroads, he suddenly heard a voice. It was like being awakened out of a deep sleep when Jan stepped up and seemed to yell in his ear.

"Hey LA, you alright?"

"Um, sure," Drake responded, but still in a daze. He continued to look around as if he saw something for the very first time. Then as quick as he was finding that thing, he noticed that Jan had brought someone with her. "Kate, we found you!"

Kate looked at Jan, then at Drake. "You let her call you LA? I thought that only I could call you by that name?"

But Drake was still looking around at the different faces in the crowd as if he was looking for something. He never found what he was looking for. It wasn't there to be found. In his thoughts, he was finally able to find the words he was searching for. There didn't seem to be a look of happiness or friendliness on the face of anyone in the entire town. He even looked in the eyes of Kate and seemed to look right through her. Drake took a deep breath and then turned to Kate and grabbed her by the shoulders. Looking right into her eyes, he asked the question that had finally come to his mind. "Kate, what is wrong with everyone in this town? Why is there so much sadness in the eyes of every person?"

"Not here, let's go to my house."

Chapter Thirteen – An Explanation

The walk to Kate's home didn't take long. Finding Billy wasn't hard to do either since he was hanging around the food sellers. Drake thinks he was about to steal something just as they walked up, and Drake just grabbed his hand and said, "No, Billy, not now." Billy was bothered and still hungry. He was surprised that Kate had been found. After the introductions, Kate waved her hand to signal 'Follow me'.

After they got out of the market area, just a few quick lefts and rights and they were standing in front of Kate's home. Drake had been close to figuring out where she lived, but had put the mines more towards the west of the town when it really was northwest. No doubt he would have gotten there eventually, but this was quicker.

"I'm glad I found you before you wandered around town too much and started asking too many questions."

Looking at Jan, Drake asked, "She found you?" Jan nodded. Then Drake turned to Kate, "How did you know we were here?"

"One of the merchants knew you were looking for me. He came by the house and said that you had taken some of his things and he has some of your things. He said you traveled over Grave Mountain together."

"That was Pepper. He saved our lives, but we didn't take his things. We went off to look at the town before we walked in. While we were away, he woke up and drove his cart into town. We tried to catch up but couldn't. I need to find him and thank him for helping us."

"I told him that I knew you and that it didn't sound like you to steal things. He stays not too far from here at night when he's in town, and we'll find him later today so you can explain all that to him. Drake, I know you live by your rules, and that you don't take things that aren't yours."

"You know, sometimes I wish you had never told me about these rules. Life might be a little easier if there weren't so many rules."

"Everybody needs lines. Rules make things easier. A life with no rules is harder than living with the rules." Billy was quiet during this entire time, but he was listening closely. He might have openly disagreed, but he had only just met Kate.

"So tell me about this town and what is happening here."

And Kate began to talk. First, she told about how they had come to move here because her Dad needed to have a job. He had heard that they were opening up the gold mine on the other side of Grave Mountain and within one day, he had decided to move away. Kate's dad had been told that the earlier a person began to work the mine, the more of a share they would have in the gold that the mine produced. There were a lot of people who showed up for those early shares. But when they got to the mine, it was soon discovered that things were not as they were led to believe.

The gold was being brought to the top of the mine and being refined inside the mine. At first, no one was sure how or who was mining the gold, but there were rumors that the Head of the Mine, a man by the name of Tunis Furbush_was using dragons to locate and mine the gold. At this point, Billy jumped in.

"Some dragons can smell gold through solid rock," Billy said.

"That is exactly right. You must be Drake's dragon expert?" Kate smiled. She hadn't smiled much. Billy looked a little embarrassed to have been noticed and to have been called an expert about anything.

"That's me." And just like that, he smiled at Jan and Drake as if to say something. Not sure what.

Kate continued. "Pepper mentioned you."

Billy didn't really like the thought that someone depended on him, mainly because it was so rare.

Kate continued, "As time progressed, it was getting more and more obvious that Furbush was not going to permit anyone else to get rich off the mine, but by the time people realized this, everyone refused to believe that they had worked so hard only to be swindled by such a smooth-talking thief as Tunis. The anger of the town grew until the workers met at the gold mine one morning, insisting that Tunis give them their share of the work they had done. Tunis got angry, very angry and returned to the crowd with a small but very impressive Torch.

He held it up above everyone as he addressed the crowd, and asked for the spokesperson for the miners to come up and discuss the issue with him. As the leader stepped forward, Tunis pointed the Torch at the man and cried out something, and a dragon flew up from the depth of the gold mine, grabbed the spokesperson, lifted him high above the crowd, and on Tunis' command, dropped him to the floor in the large cavern of the gold mine. He has not walked since that day. Rumor is that he has not slept either."

No one stirred as Kate took a moment, collected her thoughts and continued.

"Everyone has been told that Tunis commands the dragons, but how could a person have command over a dragon?"

"Well, that might be possible." Billy said rather quickly.

Everyone turned and looked at Billy, who had been fairly quiet until now. Drake was the one who broke the silence and asked him simply, "How?"

"Remember when we were talking about legends of the dragons? One very old legend was that dragons aren't born with the flame within their own bodies, but that they have to go and get it ignited when they are old enough to handle dragon fire. The heat of a dragon's flame would consume a dragon if they are too young to contain it. They have to wait until the lining of their second stomach has matured enough to contain the flame. So legend says they go to the dragon king, who is the Keeper of the Flame, to get their flame lit. To receive their flame, they must pledge their service to the Keeper of the Flame. It is one of the few ways that dragons were believed to have any social network or knowledge about their history. The Keeper of the Flame is usually the oldest and most knowledgeable dragon. He teaches young dragons about the guidelines and dangers of being a dragon."

"What makes this flame of the Keeper of the Flame so unique?"

"Well, it's just legend that I don't know is proven, but he who possesses --" and Billy stopped short. His face went a little pale and his eyes opened very wide.

"He possesses what?" Everyone wanted to know.

Billy spoke very slowly and very deliberately. "He who possesses the flame from the center of the mountain, which is also called --". Billy stopped, looked around and then Jan, Drake, and Billy all turned to Kate and the three said in unison, "The Deepest Mountain Flame!"

"You all knew about this?" Kate was visibly upset.

"No, we heard about this on our way over the pass," Billy replied.

Drake was the first to say what everyone was thinking. "Then Tunis does control the dragons. Each dragon must come to him to have his flame lit, and Tunis is using this power to make them his slaves and to work the mines for gold."

"We can't fight against Tunis if he controls one dragon or many dragons. Dragons can defeat armies and we are just a few."

"We won't fight Tunis; we will get control of the Deepest Mountain Flame and free the dragons."

Billy had to say something. "Now that's just crazy. We can't free the dragons. I thought we came here to help Kate. Who even needs the dragons to be free? As for me, I'm glad that somebody has control of them."

Drake spoke like a plan was already developing in his mind. "Can't you see that the only way to help Kate is to free her Dad from this slavery? Since her Dad is one of the miners, you would have to free them all. The reason the miners can't escape is because Tunis holds them hostage, as well as the dragons. The only reason Tunis can hold them hostage is because he controls the dragons. If we free the dragons, Tunis has no more power over the people of this town."

"But how are you going to free the dragons?"

Drake noticed that the "we" had moved to "you" pretty quick. He moved it again. "We just need to get our hands on that Torch that Tunis has. That's the key." He made it sound so simple that everyone thought he had a plan. Plans are something you have when you have time to work out all the details. Drake didn't have that kind of time and besides, this was an adventure. Adventures usually start with a plan and they become adventures when a new plan has to be figured out.

"The first part of our plan is that Billy has to teach me as much as he can about dragons, and we are going to need some lunch."

Billy was surprised he hadn't thought of lunch sooner. It was close to two hours past lunch time.

Chapter Fourteen – The Plan

As everyone began to gather around the table, Drake and Billy were off to the side, so that Billy could teach Drake as much as possible about dragons; but it was like cramming for a test. Drake didn't like to cram for tests. He preferred to do his studying slow and steady. His best days were days that he felt prepared. This was not to be one of those days. The more Billy had to say, the more Drake realized he wasn't going to make this work. At a certain point, Drake realized this, too, and then began to talk to Billy about the revised plan.

"Billy, there is just too much for me to learn in a short time. If I get something wrong, Tunis will know right away that I'm not who I say I am. The moment he suspects anything, he'll have one of the dragons pick me up and drop me just like he did with the miner."

"Well, I'm glad you finally realized this too. You've been getting things wrong since we started talking about dragons. I was wondering if you had myths and truth confused, or just couldn't see the difference between a Naga and the Chuvash dragon."

Drake was shaking his head. "I can't."

Billy let out a long breath with a bit of a moan thrown in, just for good measure, which didn't help Drake at all. He shook his head back and forth and paused. "We need another plan!" Billy still wasn't willing to give up.

Drake, thinking that cowboys don't quit, said thoughtfully: "Same plan, different person. Billy, you are going to have to come along as the expert on dragons." Drake expected Billy would resist and need some convincing. It wasn't the first, nor the last time he was wrong about Billy.

"I figured as much. It took you a little longer to realize what I already knew when we started this plan. Let's eat while you fill everyone else in."

Drake and Billy joined Jan and Kate who were already talking like they were old friends who hadn't seen each other in a long time. In fact, that is exactly what they were. Catching up on stories that mattered to old friends and different parts of the home-town that Kate had never wanted to leave. They both looked up as the boys joined them at the table. Kate was the first to ask the question.

"So Billy, is Drake an expert in the knowledge of dragons yet?"

"He doesn't have to be, we have a change in how we're going to get close to Tunis."

"Already changing plans, this doesn't sound good."

Drake took over the conversation from this point. "It is better than before. There is no possible way that I can learn all that Billy already knows about dragons. He is the expert and there is no other way to deal with that. So Billy and I will go to Tunis together. I'll be the person who is Billy's friend, and I'll introduce him to Tunis, saying that he didn't want to talk to Tunis, but I forced him. We are going to come up with information about dragons that will somehow change Tunis' approach, but we're not sure what that is just yet. First, we have to impress on Tunis the value of Billy's knowledge about dragons. We have to establish Billy, in Tunis' eyes, as an expert on all things that have to do with dragons and the legends of dragons. Then when we tell him news that might get him to rethink what he's doing, or even set him off balance for a few moments, he will respect that information. When Tunis has his guard down, we will get our hands on that Torch."

Drake looked around and there didn't seem to be anyone willing to object.

Kate and Jan looked at each other. "What did you want us to do?"

"We need you to find out who is working with Tunis, and where he gets the things he needs. He has to eat and do something while he's not working at the gold mine. We need as much about his schedule and patterns as possible in the next 24 hours. Talk to people who know him and people who live around him."

"Sounds possible. Most of this I already know." Kate replied. "It's not a very large town."

"There is one other thing that I need you to do. This might be the hardest part of all. I need you both to put yourself within earshot of Tunis and talk about Billy, the new expert in town on dragons. It will save us a lot of work if Tunis has already heard of Billy before we talk to him. You need to talk about his knowledge of dragons without letting Tunis know you are trying to let him hear you. He needs to believe that over-hearing you is completely his good fortune, and that you are not planting the idea in his head. We have to hope that Tunis is more mean than smart."

"Oh, he's plenty mean," Kate whispered under her breath, just loud enough for everyone to hear.

Chapter Fifteen – The New Expert

The more the girls thought about how to get close to Tunis, the more it seemed unlikely that he would listen to a couple of young girls, talking about some other young boy. They knew they couldn't even approach Tunis directly because he was more prone to ignore everyone than he was to listen to them talk. He didn't think that he needed to listen to others, but since he was in charge, people should be listening to him. His casual visits were limited because he held so much power in the town. He often assigned someone to do just about everything for him, except for eating his meals and sleeping in his bed at night. He was tirelessly spending time at the gold mine, which meant he usually wasn't available during the day, and they needed to find a guaranteed way to catch his ears in the next 24 hours. When he did get out in public, he was often in places reserved for adults, and the girls knew before they could catch Tunis' ears, they would most likely catch someone's eyes for being in any of the adult places Tunis liked to visit. On second thought, this looked a little harder than they thought at first.

 As they sat at the table, they decided to make a list of all the places they knew Tunis went, and find a way they could drop the hints that needed to be dropped. As they walked through the day, they couldn't find a single place they could rely on to be within earshot of Tunis. So rather than spend all their time on Tunis, they started thinking about all the people who already had access to Tunis. At the mine, it would be hard to find anyone, because those who worked at the mine had to be there longer and work harder than Tunis. The people at work that he knew and trusted just about lived at the gold mine. In fact, a few of them did. They thought that if they devoted themselves to Tunis, they were assuring their family a higher place in the town. It didn't matter if they disliked the man, but each man did what they did for their families. So as Jan and Kate reviewed the names of each of the leaders, they didn't see a way for anyone in this group to be approached.

Then Kate and Jan listed all the people who ran errands and made Tunis' life simpler. Most of the people who lived like servants were happy to make a little extra income and not have to work in the gold mine. Many of these were the wives of the men who worked in the mine, and were so frightened of losing this extra money that they would never consider being a part of a plan to overthrow the man who was spoken of in private as the little dictator of Nowhere. But the question remained, who in Tunis' life could tell him about Billy's expertise with dragons?

Who does Tunis listen to? The only people they could think of were Tunis' wife and Tamera, his daughter. Those were the only people that Kate and Jan thought they could possibly get close to. And although it might be easy to talk to them, it was not going to be enjoyable. No one in Nowhere could endure either one for very long.

First, there was Mrs. Furbush who knew how important she was, because she was old enough to see that her husband ran the town. She was not exactly sure how it all happened and frankly, really didn't care. She knew that she got to go to the front of every line, and get the best meat at the butcher shop, but she didn't want to know anything about why that was the case. It was a gradual thing for her as she grew accustomed to living in the top crust of the community, but there were still times she showed her manners and the politeness of her upbringing. But the moment you expected kindness or goodness from Mrs. Furbush was the moment something inside her turned sour, and was like a fruit that goes rotten on the inside long before it looked bad on the outside. She looked just fine, but something was not right. And it was as if she would leave a terrible taste in your mouth when she left. If you offended Mrs. Furbush too much, it was likely anyone you were related to that worked in the gold mine would pay the price of her irritation. She was too dangerous to try to get close to her. She didn't care what you thought of her as long as you knew she was married to the most powerful man in town.

Next, there was Tamera. Tamera was different. Oh, nobody liked her either, but she at least wanted to be liked. She wasn't raised with the same inbred set of manners as her mother. Seemed like of all the things that her mother showed her, she seemed to copy her Mother's feelings that she didn't have to feel any pity towards anyone else in the town. Like all children, she longed to be accepted by her peers, and because everyone was so frightened of her dad, no one dared to share any part of their lives with her. So it was decided, Tamera would be their target. Granted, Jan and Kate might feel bad to try to use Tamera's feelings of wanting to be liked against Tunis, but it was their best opportunity to get word to her father about Billy's dragon expertise. Bringing Tamera into their small circle wouldn't be hard, but how do they spark her interest in Billy? That was the issue now.

"I think I know, but it might require a little bit of pretending," Jan said.

"I don't mind pretending. What are you thinking?" asked Kate.

"If we pretend that we both have a crush on this new cute boy in town, and let it slip that he is very interesting, she might listen."

"That's not pretending." And Kate smiled.

"Really? You really think Billy is cute?"

"Why don't you?" Kate asked.

"He's all yours Kate. But first, we need to get Tamera interesting in meeting him."

"I can do that, and I think I know where I can find her about now – if we hurry. Let's go!"

And the two girls hollered to the boys 'We're off' as they walked out the door. The boys were busy going over the details of their plan, and Billy was continuing to try to teach Drake about dragons.

"Report back as soon as you have anything," but neither one heard Drake's comment. At least, they didn't act as if they had heard it. Sometimes, you can't tell if people who are already out the door really heard you or not.

As soon as they were walking down the street, Jan asked Kate where she hoped to find Tamera, but Kate was walking so fast, Jan was soon out of breath. She had to either walk with Kate or talk with Kate because there wasn't enough air in her lungs to do both. Few people walked as fast as Kate when she was strolling, but when she was in a hurry, she walked faster than some people ran. They walked into town and headed straight for the center. The market was still going strong even though some of the sellers were packing up their goods and closing shop for the day. This actually made getting through this part of town even harder as carts and such were making their way down the center of the street and people were heading in all directions at once.

While they were almost running through the busiest part of the market, Jan happened to look to the side, and she saw Pepper. Not having the time to stop and explain what had happened, she put her head down hoping that he didn't see her, but she heard him call out her name. She acted like she didn't hear him and continued to follow

Kate, all the while feeling very guilty about not at least saying hi to someone who had saved her life and the lives of her team. Just as they were rounding a corner, she looked back to see if he was still there and they locked eyes for just a moment, and Jan knew that Pepper had seen her look back at him. At that moment, someone walked in front of Jan and she walked right into them, almost knocking her down. The person she ran into was an older man and she stopped to pick up what she had knocked out of his arms.

Someone else jumped to help pick up the things that had been knocked on the ground, and then turned to her "Young lady, don't you watch where you're walking?"

"I'm so sorry; I didn't mean to run into you. I thought I saw someone I knew in town." Jan answered.

"If you know anyone in town, then you know who you just ran into." But at the moment, the person she had knocked over moved his hand towards the person who spoke as if to tell a dog to sit.

He turned slowly towards Jan.

"Young girl, what is your family name?" he asked softly as if he was commanding an answer.

"It's Harcase," Jan said, saying the first family name that came into her mind that was not hers. She could see him searching his mind for someone he knew with that name. It sounded so familiar. So she quickly added, "I'm not from around here, I'm just visiting. I have to go find my friend, I am afraid I lost her." And Jan quickly ran the direction she last saw Kate, although it seemed like Kate was not to be found.

After she had walked a short distance, Kate was suddenly beside her again.

"Where have you been, I thought I lost you!"

"Do you know who you ran into in the market? That was Tunis Furbush! You just about blew the whole plan by bringing attention to us both. We are supposed to try and keep a low profile, and you are knocking his things into the street."

"I didn't know that was him. I saw Pepper – the guy who helped us get here and worse, he saw me. I hope that doesn't come back to be any trouble to us." But somehow, Jan was pretty sure it would cause another complication in the process. So Kate walked a little slower and Jan was able to tell her the story of how they had traveled with Pepper over the pass of Grave Mountain, and how Pepper had most likely saved their lives. Pepper most likely thought Drake, Billy, and Jan had stolen some of his things just before coming to town, but Kate already knew that part of the story.

Chapter Sixteen – Tamera

The girls made quick time because they were walking at Kate's pace. In about 20 minutes, they had crossed through town. When they arrived at the drug store, Kate took a look in, and nodded at Jan as if to say the plan was on. Tamera was in the drugstore, sitting at the counter and sipping some kind of chocolate drink with whipped cream on it. By the looks of it, she had just got started on it, but Kate knew that she didn't usually finish. Tamera ate what she wanted and, because she knew she could get another one tomorrow if she wanted, she didn't feel obliged to finish. Tamera could be found in this same store, about the same time, at least three days a week. The girls were lucky to find her here because this was the fourth day this week that she was enjoying her favorite afternoon treat. It must have been a difficult week, and that could mean it would be easier to get her talking today. Of course, it could mean just the opposite. You never knew how Tamera was going to react to others.

Kate and Jan walked into the store and sat down next to Tamera without really looking directly at her. Kate and Jan started to put their part of the plan in motion.

"So what did you think about my friend? Isn't he cute?"

"He is – what brings him to Nowhere?" asked Kate.

"Well, I'm not really sure. I know we were traveling and needed to stop, and the town was here."

"What's he really like?"

"Well, he's into sports and he likes to ride his bike all over, oh and he's an expert on lots of things, especially about dragons."

Tamera's ears perked up. "Dragons?"

Kate turned to Tamera, "Oh, hi Tamera, I didn't see you there. This is my friend, Jan. Jan, meet Tamera. She is the daughter of the man who runs the mine where my dad works. Tamera, meet Jan who is from the town I used to live in before we moved to Nowhere."

Jan spoke first. "You live here? It's nice to meet you. What do you do for fun in this town?"

"Not much really, there is a place to go swimming." Tamera had never been there, but she knew other kids swam and had fun there, but she never felt very welcome among other kids. "And some places to eat, but there really isn't much of anywhere that's super fun."

"Well, we don't plan to stay too long. We just dropped in to say hi to Kate."

"Did I see you coming into town, with two boys early this morning?" asked Tamera.

"That was probably us – we made quite a mess trying to jump over the creek. As you can tell by my shoes, we didn't completely clear the water or the mud, jumping over that creek that was between the hill and the town." Jan laughed as she looked down at her shoes. "But the boys were even worse than me."

"What size shoe do you wear?"

"I think I'm a size six and a half. Why?"

"Why don't you come by my house – I've got lots of shoes and I'm a six and a half just like you. I don't think my Mom would care if I loaned you a pair." Tamera sounded actually nice, and happy to be able to invite someone to her home.

"You are so nice – that would be really great!" Jan said with a large and friendly smile.

Jan was a very good actress because this was not at all what Kate and she had planned to happen. Drake was prone to say that plans seem to remake themselves. But he didn't mention how uncomfortable the remade plan becomes when it's being remade.

Tamera didn't seem to notice if there was a hint of restraint in Jan's voice but added simply, "Follow me." As she walked out the door, Jan and Kate looked at each other and raised their eyebrows as if to say, 'I guess this is how our plan is going to go'.

Tamera led them out of the drugstore, but instead of heading straight to her house, she waved her hand at a large, fancy horse-drawn covered carriage that was close by. The driver went from being relaxed, to sitting up like he was about to play a piano that wasn't there. He smoothly stepped down from the driver's perch and opened the door for Tamera, all smiles until she passed, and then the smile quickly dropped from his face, although his voice remained happy.

"Are these girls coming along with you, Tamera?"

Tamera never looked at him but with a twinge of anger in her voice, snapped "Of course they are, why else would I be leading them into the carriage? Take us to my house."

The driver turned and nodded at the girls, and appeared surprised when they smiled at him with a kinder smile than he had seen in a long time. He returned the smile, but then there was something in his eyes that questioned why these two girls, who appeared nice, would be traveling with Tamera, who he knew to be not so very nice. In the end, he gently closed the door behind them, and slid back up in the driver's seat to begin the short trip to the Furbush home. A trip that was made even shorter by the fact they got a carriage ride, right up to the door of the mansion.

Chapter Seventeen – Dinner at Furbush's

The Furbush house was different than anything Kate or Jan had ever seen. Oh sure, Kate had seen it from a distance, but never up close. The strange thing was that it was as if all the things had been bought without a central plan in mind. The color of the lampshade was completely at odds with the color of the carpet, which didn't match the couch or the area rug, which didn't match any of the other parts either.

Upon entering the house, the housekeeper was surprised to see anyone else coming in with Tamera. So surprised that she nearly shut the door before Jan and Kate had walked through it.

Tamera didn't ask her parents if she could invite the two to dinner, she told them that she had invited Jan and Kate to dinner. It was very obvious who was in charge between her mother and her. However, with her Dad, you could see that she had to approach things differently. As the girls followed Tamera through the front room, down the hall, and into the library, Tamera was obviously looking for someone or something, but she didn't bother to inform Jan and Kate what that was. Finally, as she came to the dining room, she slowed her pace and stood there for just a moment. She turned to Kate and Jan and said:

"Just stand here and don't say anything."

Walking up to the door, the girls did as they were told, and that is where they stood when Tamera started talking to her father while he still had his back to Tamera.

"Dad, I have invited a few friends to join us for dinner."

Without turning around, he told her —"Well, un-invite them. You know I don't like sharing dinner time with anyone else. Did you and Mother both agree to this?"

"Mom knows. And I think you might want to meet them."

Still not turning around, he answered: "Why would I want to meet any of your friends?"

"They have a friend who is visiting the town, and their friend is an expert on", and she paused for effect here, "dragons." And Tamera let that sentence hang in the air for a little while like she was holding up a bright diamond to brilliant light, permitting the importance of what she just said to soak into her father's ears. She knew he was interested, when he slowly turned around and looked first at Tamera, then at Jan and Kate.

He squinted a little as he looked first at Kate, then at Jan. His eyes fixed on Jan, and his stare seemed a little deeper and longer at her. He just nodded a very slight nod of recognition and then turned back to Tamera and continued their conversation.

"Who mentioned dragons?" Furbush asked, in a little more than a whisper.

"Jan and Kate were talking about their friend, saying how he was really cute and all. I heard them even though they weren't talking to me. And all of a sudden, they mentioned that he was an expert on dragons, and I thought this is somebody you might want to talk to."

"You just heard them, where?" Mr. Furbush lifted one eyebrow and looked at Jan and Kate like people often do when they are suspicious.

"At the drugstore – when I was having my afternoon snack."

Mr. Furbush turned to Jan directly and looked her in the eyes. Squinted a little and asked, "Aren't you the girl who nearly knocked me over in the market this afternoon?" He sounded as though he was going to make this a difficult point of the conversation.

"Yes sir, I'm sorry I was chasing Kate and I took my eyes off where I was going. I hope I didn't hurt you."

"Hurt me! " In a voice that turned from irritation to kindness in less than a breath. "Of course not, I just didn't recognize you. You said you were from out of town. Hardcast is your family name?"

"No sir, I said Harcase, from the other side of Grave Mountain."

"Hmm, not many people call it Grave Mountain, except people who live on this side of the mountain." Mr. Furbush had taken to looking around the room as if he were lost in thought, or at least thinking through something on his mind. "So, you have a friend who is an expert on dragons? Are you part of the group of kids that walked into town early the other day? How do you know he is an expert on dragons? Is there some kind of dragon school that I have never heard about?" Mr. Furbush had asked four questions and never given the girls the chance to answer any one of them.

"Yes, Yes, Well, sir, that's about all he talks about, if he's not talking about food or riding his bike. And not that I know of."

"What kind of answer is that?"

"Yes, our friend is an expert on dragons. Yes, we are the kids who walked into town the other day. That is all that he talks about. No, I haven't heard of a dragon school."

Furbush just looked into Jan's eyes. "What has he told you about dragons?"

So Jan began to try to remember some of the information Billy had shared when they were all crossing Grave Mountain under the cover of the tarp in Pepper's cart. She figured she was mixing up some of the things and that didn't really matter since she was not the expert, but just telling Mr. Furbush what she could remember. With each small tidbit, he became more and more interested. Some of the information he might have known, and would nod up and down while Jan was telling her part, but some of it was new. As if someone was explaining something completely different, that made other details fall into their correct place. He even tilted his head to the side a few times and mumbled something to himself as if to say, "I didn't know that."

It didn't take too long for Jan to go through all that she remembered, because she wasn't telling it in the depth and detail that Billy had while they traveled. She didn't even try. Billy was supposed to be the expert and she wasn't. Just as she was about to say that was about all she knew, she remembered a small comment that Billy had mentioned about dragons not being that social except for when they were seeking their fire. Mr. Furbush froze and leaned into Jan as soon as she mentioned this.

"What else did he say about their fire?"

Knowing that Tunis Furbush was exactly where Jan needed him to be, she said she didn't remember too much about that. She said how she must have fallen asleep right in the middle of that part of what Billy was talking about. And then she told Mr. Furbush that when she woke up, Billy was still talking about dragons, but she had no idea how much she missed, and what else might have been said.

When Jan finished, Tunis Furbush just stood there as if someone had hypnotized him, and left him standing straight up. You could tell he was still breathing, but you had to look closely to be sure. His eyes had moved toward the window, and he was putting something together in his mind. He took a deep breath, turned to Jan and Kate and spoke as if they worked for him in his gold mine.

"You have to go get Billy and invite him for dinner tonight."

Tamera was surprised. "We can't get him here in time for dinner, it's almost dinner time right now. I don't want to eat dinner late."

Furbush looked at his daughter and shook his head. In a mildly sarcastic voice, he said, "You're not going to starve – take these girls with you, and tell the carriage driver to help you find this Billy, and bring him back here so we can have him over for dinner." He was attempting to sound polite for the sake of Jan and Kate, but it was an order and in his voice was the impression that Billy wouldn't have any choice about joining the Furbush's for dinner.

"But Dad!"

He cut her off – "Do it now! We'll have dinner waiting for you all when you get back. And bring him back with you or don't come back." There was a threat in the tone of Tunis Furbush's voice, but neither Jan nor Kate knew what was behind that threat. It was obvious that Tamera did, because her steps got quicker, and she wiped the tear away that had begun to form in her eye.

For a moment, Kate thought that she was beginning to understand a little more of what the life of Tamera was really like. Sometimes when you know someone who can order a chocolate sundae any day of the week, you might think their life is pretty good. It might bother you that they seem to have everything they want, and you even might dislike them just because they can do whatever they want when they want. Then you start to understand what their life is really like. You begin to have more understanding for them, and know why they act the way they do. Jan was beginning to understand the other side of Tamera Furbush.

Chapter Eighteen – Getting into Furbush's Home

"I hope you know where we can find this friend of yours."

Tamera's attitude had definitely taken a turn for the worse. It was then that Kate and Jan realized that they were not working their plan, but Tamera was working hers. They hadn't known that Tamera was on specific instructions from her father to be aware of anyone who arrived from out of town, especially if that person said they knew anything about dragons. Billy met both qualifications. That command was given months ago, and although she had kept her ears open, Tamera had not found anyone her Dad would find interesting until now. There had been a lot of people who came into town that were new. Some were looking for work, some were selling their wares at the local market and some were just passing through. But this was the first time Tamera had actually heard anyone mention anything about dragons. Tamera knew that if she were successful, her dad would be happy with her and she could buy a few more things that she wanted.

Kate was the first to speak. "Is something wrong, Tamera?"

Tamera turned to Kate, her eyes initially had anger in them with just a touch of fire, but then it was as if a quick and powerful wind that no one could feel blew that fire out and she became at once, the soft-spoken person that had led them from the drugstore to her carriage and then to her home.

"Of course not, - my father just puts me a little off balance when he screams at me like that. I hope he didn't frighten you because he really is very kind."

Kate knew Tamera was now lying about her father because the rumors in the mill were enough to tell you that no one in town was as mean-tempered as Tunis Furbush. She looked over at Jan who smiled. She remembered the stories that Kate had told them while they were eating, and that look from Kate was meant to help keep Jan on her guard against the entire family.

"So do you know or not?"

"Know what?" asked Kate, having forgotten the question.

"Do you know where to find this friend of yours?"

"Oh sure, just head over to my house" – said Kate. When Tamera rolled her eyes and Kate added as if she intended all along – "which is between the town and the gold mine, but towards the Northwest a little."

As Kate said that, Jan remembered back to the first time she got Kate's letter, and the confusion they had to understand those few words, which now make such perfect sense. Remembering back, it was easy to remember what they didn't know then. They didn't know about Grave Mountain or even that Nowhere was the name of the town. They didn't know about the gold mine, they didn't even know that 'mine' was a place. They didn't know about the danger that might be in this adventure, or that going over the mountain pass would be so dangerous. Most of all, they didn't know that the dragons were for real. By the time Jan got through thinking about what she didn't know, the carriage was almost in front of Kate's house, and you could see people coming out of their homes to see what could possibly bring such a fancy carriage into this part of town.

It suddenly occurred to Jan that somehow she and Kate would have to bring the guys up to speed with all that had happened since they left Kate's house earlier today, but that was going to be almost impossible with Tamera there. Once again, the plan and the adventure were becoming uncomfortable. Jan's mind was running wild with ideas about how to do this when Tamera's voice interrupted her thoughts.

"Jan, did you hear me?"

"Um no, I didn't. What did you say?"

"Really, I don't know why I bother telling people anything at all if they don't listen. I said – do you think you and Kate should go in first and let your friends know they are coming to dinner at the Furbush's house. You might have to explain who we are and what an honor it is to come to our home."

Kate jumped in – "That's a really good idea, Tamera. Can you give us just a few minutes?"

"Alright but not many. I still haven't eaten dinner, and I'm very hungry. Hurry up and make them, um I mean invite them to come to our house for dinner."

"We'll be out as soon as we can with both of them," answered Kate as they both jumped from the carriage and walked inside.

Jan could see the boys watching the carriage through the window, and Kate looked around the neighborhood. Everyone was staring at the Furbush's fancy rig. Kate wanted to apologize to those who knew her for even talking to someone in the Furbush family, but there was no time. Jan wanted to get in the house as quickly as possible and help the guys to follow her lead, at least for this part of the plan.

No sooner had she entered the house than the other members of the team began to ask questions and Jan was the one that held up both her hands as if to say stop and listen. Then she said, "We only have a few seconds, let me tell you where we are." She quickly explained that as soon as Furbush heard there was an expert on dragons, he wanted to meet with that person. Something was obviously bothering the man in terms of what was next when dealing with dragons. Dragons can be sneaky beings – you think you are in charge, and then at some moment that they determined long ago, they change everything around and you go from being their Master to being their lunch in moments. Dragons have a lot of patience when it comes to making and keeping a plan. You are never safe when your future includes trusting a dragon, let alone more than one dragon. Alone they are clever and dangerous, but collectively they are lethal and cruel. Their plans come about slowly and steadily as if to lure their prey into a false sense of security until it is too late. Maybe that was what Tunis Furbush had come to realize?

Kate broke in. "We need to get moving before Mr. Furbush gets upset. I will tell you about all of this during the trip there, while we're traveling back to their house. What you really need to know is that Tunis Furbush has been waiting for someone like you to come to this town."

Billy raised his eyebrows and looked across the room, slowly stopping on each set of eyes to see if they were thinking what he was thinking. Drake was the first to mention what had crossed the mind of everyone. "I'm not very comfortable with that." Cowboys are known to understate how they really felt, and Drake was no different. Drake was very nervous about the fact that Tunis Furbush had been looking forward to seeing them before they even knew they were coming. Their plan felt like somebody else was in charge of the whole thing from the very beginning.

Drake took the lead once again. "Well, we better accept the fact that this plan has a mind of its own, and get going over to meet Tunis Furbush. We've come too far to quit now." He was again the leader of what was left of the plan to help Kate's family escape from the work in the gold mine.

Chapter Nineteen – Meeting Tunis

The ride back to the Furbush's home was spent listening to Tamera complain about how late dinner would be that night. She complained to no one in particular, but got a little more angry when she realized no one in particular was listening to her. It was her opinion, shared by no one else, that she deserved to be listened to. But everyone knows that just because you hold an opinion, doesn't mean it's true.

Kate and Jan were too nice to completely ignore her. They also thought the boys could use the extra time they had to get their thoughts together about what they were going to tell Furbush and what they were going to try and hide from him. One of the problems was that Drake was not at all prone to hiding the truth. Billy told him that if the subject didn't come up, then he wouldn't have to lie about it. However, if it did come up and you asked Drake a clear and concise question, he would give the answer as he knew it to be. That might prove to be a difficulty. Billy knew this might happen and was ready to step in if needed. That was one more reason why he would be put out front as the dragon expert. He had a little bit of that same craftiness running through the blood in his veins that runs in the veins of dragons.

"So which one of you two is the dragon expert?" asked Tamera.

Billy spoke up quickly to help keep Drake from telling more of the truth than he needed to tell: "We both are." With not the slightest inclination of doubt in his voice.

"Wow – my dad is looking forward to talking to both of you." And then almost to herself, she whispered, "This should really be nice for me." She looked around just as these words left her mouth as though no one was supposed to hear that last comment. It was then she realized that the carriage had stopped and there was no more outside noise covering those softly spoken words. Now, in the quiet of the evening, you could hear the horses breathing and the driver descending from the seat where the carriage driver sat. You could even hear the steps of Mr. Furbush as he walked up to the carriage and opened the door.

"Welcome to my home – won't you please come in and have dinner with me and my family." With a smile that was just a little too big and words just a little too sweet, the kids all knew this was not going to be as simple as they supposed. Trying to hide her pointing finger as they entered the house, Tamera indicated that both Drake and Billy were the two that Mr. Furbush would be most interested in talking to. But both Jan and Kate saw it.

Mr. Furbush led the entire group towards the dinner table, and the smell of the food seemed to hit all of them like the rush of a dream that you can't wait to begin. They had been so busy throughout the day that food had been only a passing thought. Billy had forgotten he was hungry until he stood in front of the table and saw the feast that had been laid out for them. Much to the dismay of Tamera, she was not at either one of the places of honor near the head of the table. These spots were reserved for the two visiting dragon experts, Drake and Billy. It was very clear that Mr. Tunis Furbush had his reasons for wanting them in his house, but if they couldn't find out what Mr. Furbush's purposes were, things could go very bad. Very bad indeed.

"Where are those servants? You'll have to excuse us, but we were all so busy getting ready for the extra guests that we are just a little unprepared." There was a twinge of irritation and rise of volume in Mr. Furbush's voice as he looked around for the servants, who came in quickly when they heard him raise his voice. "Serve our guests," he barked, and then smugly looked at the visitors and added, "Please" as more of an afterthought.

With fear in their eyes that was not missed by any of the group, the servants hurried to get the food on the plates of all who sat around the table. As soon as each person was properly served, Mr. Furbush nodded at the servants, who then left the room, and he announced the beginning of the meal with a simple, "Enjoy your meals – umm please." And as everyone's attention was turned to the food, Tunis Furbush turned to the boys and asked a very direct question, "So which one of you two is the dragon expert?"

Billy's mouth was already chewing on food, and although he was hungry, he wasn't crude. He tried to swallow as quickly as possible, but Drake spoke up first.

"Billy is the true expert. I have been learning as much as possible from him, but he knows more about dragons than any book I have ever read about dragons."

This was actually quite clever because Drake had never read any books about dragons. Everything he knew had been learned from Billy. And Billy was impressed that Drake didn't spill the whole plan. He had told the truth and not gone too much further. And so Tunis Furbush turned to Billy and said very coolly, "Tell me what you know about dragons, boy."

Billy swallowed and looked over to Drake with a quick look, hoping that Mr. Furbush didn't catch the glance. "This might take some time Mr. Furbush."

"I've got all the time we need – tell me what you know."

And so Billy set down his fork, wiped his mouth with his tattered sleeve, and begin to tell Tunis Furbush the information that he and Drake had reviewed. The plan was to give Furbush enough information about dragons to convince him that Billy knew what he was talking about, but not enough to be considered dangerous. It was a thin line to be sure, mainly because they were still learning to understand the temperament of Mr. Furbush. The goal was to attempt to look as though they were here by chance, and that they could be of help to Mr. Furbush in dealing with the dragons. They did not want him to know that they had come to free Kate's family from the servitude of the gold mine.

After about 45 minutes of talking with Mr. Furbush, and Billy sometimes giving the lead to Drake so Billy might get a bite in, Mr. Furbush was so significantly impressed with both the boys, that he seemed to relax and begin eating his own dinner. There was generally a lighter feeling in the air as they each finished their meals.

"So, what are your plans while you're here in town?" asked Mr. Furbush.

Jan took the lead on this question. "We plan to leave tomorrow. We have to get back home because our summer is coming to an end. We were just here to visit Kate. She's from our town on the other side of Grave Mountain." Saying they were leaving tomorrow was a bit of a risk because if Mr. Furbush didn't take the bait, they would have to leave with the task of freeing Kate's family still undone, and that would never sit well with Drake or Jan.

"I have something I'd like to show the boys before they leave. Can you meet me here early tomorrow morning?"

Turning to the rest of the group, Drake raised an eyebrow as if to pose a question, and when Jan nodded, he replied, "Sure, we'll be here early tomorrow. What is it you'd like us to see?"

"I think you'll both be interested. Meet me here early."
And with that, he walked towards the back of the house
and bid everyone a good night.

Chapter Twenty – Furbush's Story

Since everyone had to walk home that night, they all got back late and tired. Not being sure just what the plan was, and not knowing what "early" meant to Mr. Furbush, the boys woke and got out of bed before the sun rose. Drake was prone to get up early, but Billy was not very friendly early in the day. Truth is, normally Billy was not very friendly at all, but he had been slowly changing during the whole trip. With the anticipation of seeing living dragons, he was enthusiastic when he remembered what was on the schedule for the day.

The boys started to walk towards the Furbush's home, when after going just a few hundred yards, they saw the family carriage coming around the corner. Nothing had been said about getting picked up, but when they looked inside the carriage, only Mr. Furbush was there. They noticed for the first time that on the side of the carriage there was a crest with the outline of a younger Tunis Furbush, and a touch of something in his hands. Faintly, you could see several shadows in the picture, although it was not clear what they were unless you knew what you were looking for. They were shadows of dragons flying around the head of Tunis. Billy pointed at the crest as they approached the carriage, and Drake nodded as though he had already seen it.

"Well, get on in here and let's head over to the mine. I have a few things to show you, and a few questions to ask you about dragons. I might need your help with some information."

"Are those dragons on your family crest outside the door?"

"They are – not everyone catches that."

"Did I see four shadows?"

"There are only three now, but I don't need to have the crest redrawn, since no one knows that but me, and now you two know that one has died as well. I didn't even tell my wife."

That confirmed Drakes suspicion that the dragon that had died at Francis' home recently was indeed one of those dragons under the service of Tunis Furbush. That dragon had been burned by Deepest Mountain Flame. This also confirmed to both of them that Tunis had somehow come into possession of the Flame and he was using it to control the dragons. He was also most likely using the dragons to control the people who worked in the Gold Mine through fear. No one would resist a person who controlled dragons, especially if he was inclined to be cruel and harsh, which is exactly how Tunis Furbush was down to his very core. At least that was how it appeared to most. Drake wasn't 100 percent sure about this. Not too much more was said while the carriage traveled to the mine, but you could see that something was on Furbush's mind. It was as if there was a riddle that he had not solved yet, so he sat in silence. Both boys could sense that he was trying to work out something, without any luck.

It seemed like about 30 minutes before the carriage stopped in front of the large cave that led into the mountain. The carriage had passed people walking towards the mine, but the morning shift wouldn't begin for another hour, and no one was permitted to enter the mine unsupervised. No one except Mr. Furbush and his guests. Everyone walked calmly past the guards with the only indication that all was okay being a slight wave of the hand by Mr. Furbush. Everyone knew Tunis Furbush by sight, and knew better than to question him when he was entering the mine. No part of the mine was considered off-limits to Tunis or his guests.

Entering the mine at this time of the day was unusual. Although the outside air was cold, the air just inside the mine was warmer and in fact, there was a warm breeze coming from the depth of the mine as the warmer air below naturally rose towards the cooler air. At the opening of the mine, it seemed to come like a gust, but quickly died down once they were inside. The air pressure was something you noticed as you walked through the entrance. Drake turned to Billy and saw him holding his nose, and blowing softly to even out the pressure in his ears. Almost like someone who just came up from the bottom of a swimming pool. Billy was looking all around the cave in wonder. Drake was more focused on Tunis Furbush, and where he was looking.

The descent into the mine was not very difficult, but it became evident that the source of the heat that was exiting the front entrance was coming from deep within the mine. About 15 minutes after they entered the mine, they began their climb down. Tunis stopped at a set of lockers and stepped up to the largest, nicest locker in the group. He then pulled out a large set of keys and opened the locker that had his name on it. He told the boys to give him their coats, stating as a matter of fact that they would not be needing them as they went deeper into the mine. This was a little surprising to Drake since in his experience, the deeper you got into a cave, the more you needed your coat but they both handed over their coats. Mr. Furbush closed the locker with his key, and started walking deeper into the cave. Not much was said between anyone for the next part of the trip, but the heaviness of the air and the heat of the cave began to be more and more apparent. Tunis continued down, sure of each step, confident he was aware of where they were going, all the time with something continuing to eat away in the back of his mind.

Although the mine was lit, there were still shadows behind every turn, and noises just out of reach of clearly hearing them. Voices that were either too soft or too distant to comprehend. On one occasion, Tunis held up his hand to stop the group, and just stood still listening. Tunis held his finger to his mouth as if to quiet any talking in the group. He stood perfectly still and quiet, cupping his hand to his ear to listen to the deeper parts of the mine. Almost as soon as he stopped the sounds diminished far below the level of clear comprehension. After spending perhaps two minutes in silence, he moved his finger off his lips and motioned for the boys to continue to follow him. Even when one of the boys would create a normal noise as they walked along, Tunis would turn to look, as If to yell -- but he remained perfectly quiet, making no noise. Just like when your Mom tries to tell you to be quiet when you are visiting someone else's house.

After another steady descent deeper into the cave, Mr. Tunis Furbush came to a broad door that looked as though it had been beaten by a large wooden club. He stepped up to the door and unlocked it, and led the boys inside. Then he locked the door behind him. This was not a very comfortable feeling, so Drake was the first to speak out.

"Mr. Furbush, what are we doing here?"

"Yes, -- uh, Drake is it?" Nodding his head up and down, he continued. "I thought you would be the first to speak up. I have a few questions, and I hope you and Billy can help me answer them."

"We'd be happy to answer anything we can, but did we have to come down in the mine to do that?" asked Drake.

"You did and you do. Just a few more seconds."

And with that, he pulled his huge ring of keys out of his pocket and began unlocking the locks on the thick door that appeared to lead to a smaller room off the main area. There were about 5 different locks on that door, each one requiring a different key, some twisting left and some twisting right. There was one that twisted left and then twisted right again to release the final bolt. As the door opened, it scraped against the floor, and the noise was one of those noises that makes your back and shoulders curl up. But that was hardly noticed, since within the room, there was a light that had magical qualities to it, unlike anything either boy had ever seen. It was a bright light, but it didn't create any shadows. It came from a Torch that stood on a stand in the middle of the room, and as soon as Mr. Furbush took it in his hands, it appeared as if the flame was under his control. At that same moment, there was a stirring from deep within the cavern, as if moving this Torch moved whatever was at the bottom of the gold mine caves. Now that the Torch was in the hands of Tunis, it behaved like most every Torch. The light returned to normal and the heat was only present when you were close enough to feel it. Mr. Furbush brought it out of the locked room, and out into the open.

"Don't touch the mantle of the Torch because that will be deadly."

"You brought us all the way down into this cave to see a Torch?" Drake inquired.

Billy stood in amazement and could hardly speak – when he did, he whispered: "It's true, this is the Torch of the Deepest Mountain Fire." And turning to Drake, "This is what every dragon requires if they are a fire breathing dragon."

Mr. Furbush stood and listened. He knew it was valuable to the dragons, but now he knew why. He had used this to get the dragons to cooperate with him, to dig in his mine, to find the gold and even to carry it to a higher level. That way the men would not have to work so hard to get to the gold. But Tunis never imagined that it served such a purpose!

"How did you find this?" Billy spoke without really thinking about it.

"I've always mined for gold. I was in the south and wondered why all the miners who tried to stake out claims in the lower range never returned. In my mind, it was because they were greedy and didn't want to share their gold. The rumors about the hills being full of gold, and that no one ever came back caused people to make up stories, and of course dragons were part of that. Rumor had it that the miners were eaten by the dragons, and so for centuries, no one dared to venture up to the hills. I had hit so many low points in my life that being eaten by a dragon didn't sound so bad, so one day I packed up all I had, left my wife and daughter behind, and headed out to see if there was any gold the dragon didn't want that I could find and keep."

"When I got to this mountain, it looked so much like the mountains from the old days of mining, that I thought there had to be gold here. As I entered the cave, I noticed that there was heat coming from deep within the mountain."

"I thought caves were colder than the open air."

"Usually they are unless something from within was making it warmer. I had convinced myself that there must be a dragon inside the cave. So I camped on the valley floor and watched. I noticed that there were no birds or bats that ever entered the cave, and that in the morning air, steam would rise from the mouth of the cave. Now I was sure there was something unusual about this cave. I began to consider how I could get into the deeper parts of the mine, always mindful of the legends about miners who never returned home. I camped on the outside of this mountain for months, trying to find the courage to enter. After living outside for almost two years, one day I noticed that the warmth of the mountain appeared to be diminishing."

"How could you tell?"

"Less steam in the mornings was rising. I began to notice that birds were beginning to fly into the cave again. It was as if the mountain began to welcome life again. So I planned my journey into the cave, not knowing what I would find there."

"It must have been hard to head into a cave, not sure if you'd find a dragon guarding the entrance," said Drake, who admired courage no matter the form.

Furbush could tell Drake understood what it cost him to walk into the cave that day. "I was very concerned. As you are aware, humans don't last long when they meet dragons. Humans aren't even enough to be considered a good snack for most dragons."

Billy said, matter-of-factly, "They prefer sheep and goats more than humans because most dragons have a good sense of smell. They don't like the taste of clothing. This is why most ranchers would drape old clothes over their flocks when there was a dragon rumored to be close. They usually just burn up humans because they are more bother than tasty. None the less, I'd rather not be their meal, preferred or not."

Furbush turned to Billy, as if frozen for a moment, "How did you get to know so much about dragons?"

"Just do – I study the legends and stories about them."

Furbush continued his story. "So I descended down into the cave, and when I reached the bottom, I saw a large stack of gold in bricks and stones. So large, I knew I could never get it out by myself. I was very happy until I found the dragon who owned the gold. At first, I thought he was sleeping but on closer look, I realized he had died on top of his pile of riches."

"Died of what?" asked Drake.

Both of them turned to Billy.

"What? Well, from what I've read, some dragons get old and die. Some dragons just decide to quit living, although that is very rare. Usually, they die from injuries or are killed. "

Mr. Furbush continued. "Billy is right. When I went down to the bottom of the cave, and after days of watching this dragon lay motionless, I decided to approach him. As I got closer, it was obvious that he had been impaled by something that had caused an injury that eventually killed him. As I explored the cave, it became apparent to me that the gold in this cave wasn't brought in from other places, but was mined from this mountain."

"That would not surprise me because many dragons can smell gold through miles of rock. Some are known for their ability to dig it out of the earth much like a gopher finds worms in the ground. Usually, one dragon doesn't have all that he needs to mine gold because different dragons have different skills. Some can smell gold. Some can dig it and still, others can refine it." Billy spoke as if he were reading a book, and maybe in his mind he was, but he knew about dragons.

"Hmm, that makes a lot of sense to quite a few things."

Drake was watching Furbush tell the story and asked the question that had begun this discussion. "How does all this relate to the Torch?"

"It was still burning when I found it next to the dead dragon. When I picked it up, I knew that not only did I have it, but it had me. I don't know what that means, but it has me more frightened now than ever."

Chapter Twenty-One – The DragonTorch

Drake paused as he heard a loud noise off deeper in the cave and then turned and looked at Tunis Furbush. Tunis had finished his part of what he wanted to say. Drake began to understand that Tunis was actually looking to them for help, something he never expected.

"Billy, what do you know about this Torch?"

"Most of what I have read about this Torch comes from rumors and handed down stories. Most of it was written down because these stories were only known by oral traditions, and there was concern that they would be forgotten. Some of those stories have been passed down hundreds of years, so long that no one actually remembers the events. I don't really know what is true. Tradition says that the Torch was something that was created shortly after the beginning of time, when the world was younger, and the balance of power was still in question. Dragons were the most stunning of all creatures. They had strength and size and lived centuries longer than most all the other animals of the earth. But they used their size and power to dominate other creatures, because they had no equals above or below the earth. They had nothing to keep them in check, except for their desire for more wealth and power. Because of their power, they were made by creation unable to break a promise they make. For centuries they abused their power, and enslaved most of the inhabitants of the earth, always wanting more power and more wealth."

"Knowing their desire to be all-powerful, the Power behind the Universe determined to make them an offer to give them the ability to breathe fire if they would commit to serve the Keeper of the Flame. Hungry for even greater power, their lust to control hid this gift for the real trap that it was. Being very powerful has never been a cure for wanting more power, so every dragon was required to make a pledge to receive the ability to breathe fire. The Keeper of the Flame was originally given to mankind, since mankind seemed to be able to follow directions the best, but eventually, mistakes were made and the flame fell into the possession of one of the dragons."

"A dragon can be held in service to the Keeper of the Flame for up to two years before he is required to give them their dragon fire. After two years, the agreement is considered to be excessive, and the dragons will no longer serve the Keeper of the Flame. Story is told that they turned on the last human to possess the flame, and that is the last history that was written about the DragonTorch. That was more than 3,000 years ago."

"There have been some dragons that refused to serve, which is why there are stories of non-fire breathing dragons. These are those who either could not find the Keeper of the Flame or refused to serve the Keeper of the Flame. Every dragon that wants the flame is all dependent on the Keeper's fulfillment of his responsibilities."

Tunis sat quietly and added up something in his head, all the while mumbling and nodding his head. No one knew what to say. Billy broke the silence.

"The Keeper of the Flame is supposed to make them commit to the promises written on the base of the Torch, if you can read dragon. I don't know the words, but legend says that this Torch is what saved the animals of the earth from being ruled by the dragons."

"Billy, look at the Torch. This isn't written in some strange language, it is as clear as can be."

Now Billy and Mr. Furbush turned and stared at Drake as if he had said something quite remarkable, because he had. Drake just didn't realize it yet.

"You mean the markings on the Torch?"

"Drake, can you read this text on the Torch?"

"Of course, can't you? Billy; you can read it, can't you?"

Both of them stared back at Drake as if to say they were surprised that Drake didn't know they couldn't read this. And Drake stared back at them as if he were surprised they couldn't do the same. It was Mr. Furbush that spoke first.

"No Drake, neither one of us can read it. How is it that you can?"

"I don't know – hold it up Mr. Furbush, and slowly turn it. I'll read it to you."

So Mr. Furbush stood up and held the Torch about eye level and Drake placed his finger near, but not on the Torch. Slowly Mr. Furbush turned the Torch, and Drake read the inscription that was carved carefully and cleanly into the handle of the Torch.

"Hmm, didn't notice this the first time, there are three different promises to be made here."

"Just read the words Drake"

As Drake began to read, the entire cave became suddenly still and quiet! "Drakonas ka Sakra petima, Drakenas ka putros õ Dak Falama putrosos, Drakenas ka garentos æõ Drakenos domus Terros"

Drake turned to look at the other two, as if to say he had answered their request, but neither of them had understood a word of what Drake had just read.

Billy was the first to say the obvious. "Now, would you mind telling us what you just read in a language we understand?"

Drake had no idea how he knew what he just read or how he knew what it said. It was only when he heard his own voice reading the text that he reasoned this was not just normal text. He stared at the ground, then back at Billy, then Mr. Furbush. There were questions here that he didn't have an answer to give. He did know this language, but he couldn't remember ever learning it or even hearing it. His tongue made sounds that were foreign to him and yet, sounded like he had known it for his whole life. Drake stepped back away from the three of them, and then sat on the bench in the small room, shocked more than anyone else by the words that had just come out of his own mouth. It was his voice, but he could not explain it.

Billy shouted at him - "Drake".

But Mr. Furbush held Billy back and softly said – "Give him a minute, he's more confused about this than you are."

Drake stared back at Billy with a blank stare as if to ask 'What has happened to me?" It was almost two full minutes before Drake spoke again, and the cave had remained completely quiet while they both waited for him to catch his breath.

Drake spoke softly with a trembling voice. It wasn't speaking the words that were written on the Torch that concerned him, but the fact that he could read and understand these strange letters. It was as if Drake just got the air knocked out of his lungs as his breaths were short and staggered. "The words from the Torch are the promise the dragons must make. The promise has three parts and they are: "I will not hold slaves, I will not kill for the joy of killing, I will not band with other dragons to rule the earth." But there was more that Drake did not read aloud. He wasn't even sure that he should tell the others about the rest of the writing. He couldn't sort out why or how he could read these words.

Chapter Twenty-Two – Meeting Dragons

Before Drake could figure out this new development, there was a loud, deep thud outside the small room they were in. The sound was as if a large rock had fallen from above, but it ended up being much worse than that. Drake, Billy, and Mr. Tunis Furbush all turned in unison to look at the noise, and there stood three medium-sized dragons staring into the room. For the next few moments, no one moved.

Now in case you've never stood next to a dragon, you might have thought these were full-grown dragons. Next to a full-grown man, a medium dragon is larger than a cart full of grain, and two donkeys. If you had been in full daylight, dragons are actually quite remarkable, but in a cave, where darkness rules the space, they are mainly scary. It was the largest, and presumably the oldest one who stepped forward towards the other two. As soon as this happened, Tunis held the Torch up high, and all of the dragons stopped and bowed down. The ones in the back dropped down to the ground but the older one, bowed just his head while keeping his eyes on the three humans.

He opened his mouth and Billy and Mr. Furbush heard a soft roar. But Drake heard something altogether different.

"We heard you use Dragon-speak."

Drake looked at the others and it was clear that they could not understand what this older dragon was saying.

"That was me, my name is Drake," Drake replied in a language he didn't know that he knew.

The dragon took a step forward and said, "Human Drake, are you the True Keeper of the Flame?"

This question frightened Drake because he knew the wrong answer would get everyone killed right now. The words of the dragon were civil enough, but it was apparent by the movement of his body, he was not at peace with the present situation. Tunis lifted the Flame higher and the dragon paid no attention to him, as if Tunis were holding a small stick.

"We will not serve the Keeper of the Flame any longer. The end of our time of service is at hand."

Drake would have to presume more of the story than Billy had told him.

"You will serve the full term, the promises shall be observed and the flame will be given as it is written."

All the dragons stepped back when Drake spoke these words with more authority than he actually had, and the dragons bowed down lower than before.

"Why have you waited so long to come to us?"

Drake wasn't even sure where the next response came from, but he replied with an age-old saying that is well known to dragons from birth.

"Just as dragons have no slaves, time has no master. I am here now, and you will soon see an end to your service in this mountain."

"You are not ordinary human, Drake."

Drake, who did not feel like Drake right now, bowed his head as a measure of respect and thanks for the words of the dragon. The older dragon stepped back to the others, said a few quick words, and then flew away down into the caverns below. The others looked back at Drake, and then followed the largest dragon. As they flew off, Drake could catch small phrases of their discussion, but it was not enough to piece together what they were saying. Drake knew they were talking about him, but could not hear the specifics.

Without knowing it, the other two had walked up to Drake, but Drake was not aware of their approach. Billy said it first.

"What just happened?"

"You can talk to these things?" asked Mr. Furbush.

"Drake, how come you didn't tell me you knew how to talk to dragons?" Billy was fascinated.

"Honestly Billy, I didn't know I could. I think this comes from my dreams. The more I learned about dragons from you, the more dreams I had about them. I thought it was just because it was all we talked about, but it was something more. In my dreams, I could talk to them and I guess, somehow, I learned Dragon-speak while I was dreaming."

There was silence for a moment as they could see the look on Drake's face.

"I really don't know." Drake shrugged his shoulders, raised his eyebrows and turned away from the others.

Tunis wanted to know everything that was said. He had sensed more and more in the past few months that the dragons were losing their patience with the situation, and the very last thing you want to do is make a dragon angry. Mr. Furbush had considered running away from the entire town, but leaving behind all that wealth was not in his greedy nature. This was why he had been even more on edge than normal with everyone, including his family and the people who worked for him.

"Mr. Furbush, it seems to me that everything Billy told us about the Keeper of the Flame is true. These dragons have served you for the right of earning their dragon-fire, and they are coming to the end of their time of service. I am not sure, but it seems to be just days away."

"When he said I was not ordinary, he meant that you are, and that meant you would not be able to give them the

Dragon-flame. They would have killed you for making them serve without being able to give them the flame at the end of their service. They would have taken the Torch for themselves."

Mr. Tunis Furbush did not say much.

"I believe this has already been tried, correct?"

Mr. Furbush nodded, but didn't speak as his head dropped almost in shame.

Billy looked at Mr. Furbush and then at Drake. "Drake, how did you know this?"

"It all adds up to what we were told at Francis' home when we crossed Grave Mountain. What he told us first was the end of the story. That was about the dragon dying. Now we need to know why Mr. Furbush burned him with the Flame from the Deepest Mountain."

"How did you defeat the dragon that confronted you?" asked Drake.

"I'm really not sure. The power of the Torch is the only possible reason. The first dragon that came to me had been with me for almost two years."

Billy added pretty quickly, "Dragons don't count time with a calendar, but by seasonal moons. They have four main points, based on the four seasons, and the moon is in the middle of each season."

Tunis continued. "The dragon that tried to take the Torch was not the largest, but stood before me one day and waited. When I ordered him to get to work, he said something and then began to show his anger towards me. Because of the power of the Torch, I backed him down, but he didn't stop. I wasn't sure what to do, but as I approached it, it calmed down and lay almost like a kitten on its side."

"He expected you to give him the flame he had earned by his service,"

"I didn't know that at the time. As the dragon lay on its side, I walked towards him, and then at the last minute I turned and used the flame as a weapon to burn into his body, driving it into his side. I was surprised that his armor melted away and the dragon's skin was exposed. He screamed horribly in pain and then flew away. The screaming never stopped until he was very far off into the night."

"That was how he ended up at Francis' home. Francis is known to heal any animal that requests care. He prefers animals more than people and evidently, even the dragons know of his healing power. Francis wasn't able to heal the dragon because, by the time the dragon arrived at his home, the Deepest Mountain Fire had already done too much damage to be healed. He died a few days before we arrived to spend the night."

Billy sat down as if to prepare to listen to more of the story, and then spoke his mind as he was prone to do.

"Is there anything to eat down here Mr. Furbush? I am starving."

"Yeah, he's right. We probably do need to eat something."

Chapter Twenty-Three – The Story of the Torch

The three of them had been down in the cave since early morning, and noon was quickly arriving. The work in the mine had been not as active as one would expect. Mr. Furbush explained that for the last few months, the dragons had been doing less and less as their impatience grew shorter and shorter. It had all but stopped after the incident with burning the dragon, and he was sure that they were planning on how to overtake him, kill him, and take the Torch for themselves. This was why Mr. Furbush had begun to fear for his own life, and was so open to discussing how to exit this situation. He had correctly understood that dragons could smell gold through the core of the mountain, and would most likely be able to track him down if he fled with the Torch.

Mr. Furbush did have some food stashed away, but since he hadn't spent a lot of time in the mine recently, it was a bit on the stale side, and not very tasty. However, when your stomach is empty, even old food tastes alright. You wouldn't normally choose to be eating this stale food on an average day.

After the few dried cakes had been eaten, and the water from the jugs, that somehow tasted the worst of anything they ate, was finished, they turned once again to the problem they were facing.

"Mr. Furbush, do you know when the next full moon is?"

"It's in two days, Drake."

"Billy, you said they measure time in full moons?"

"That's what the books said, but I've never talked to dragons like you have Drake."

"As far as I can guess, we have two days to figure out what to do, the earlier the better. Mr. Furbush, can you hand me the Torch?"

"I'm not going to give the Torch to you. Then you'll have complete control over the dragons, and I'll be targeted to be killed."

Drake looked back almost surprised but a little disgusted. "I'm not going to kill you. You can't make the dragons complete their pledge, but I can. You can't solve this, but I can. Give me the Torch, or you risk your life and most likely the lives of everyone in this town, even your wife and daughter."

Furbush still had to think about this, but he had realized weeks ago that he could not continue to be the Master of the dragons if they didn't willingly submit to him. Until now, he hadn't realized the time would be limited, and now he also knew it would be over soon no matter what. He looked at Billy and then at Drake, bowed his head a little, then stretched out his hand as if to give the Torch to Drake.

Just as Drake was about to take the Torch from Mr. Furbush's hand, something caught Drake's eye in the writing around the base of the Torch that stopped him from reaching out. He was frozen in his movements as he read a portion of the base of the Torch that had been hidden previously by Furbush's hand. Drake read it out loud, as if everyone else could understand what he was reading.

"Putrosa Onomas Volarat Domus Logi-Markvörður"

Billy and Furbush both looked at Drake and shook their shoulders, almost in unison. "So what does that mean?

Drake was frozen for a moment as he thought about what he had just read. Rather than take the Torch, he sat down, and both Billy and Furbush stared at him.

"Death to the One who takes this from the Torch Keeper"

"But I'm giving this to you, you aren't taking it."

"I don't think it means that – the meaning goes deeper than just those words. It means that the ownership of the Torch cannot just be handed over."

Drake turned to Billy. "Billy, do you remember anything else about the Torch in all your reading?"

"Hmm, nothing comes to mind but, no wait, let me think. Let me see," and then he closed his eyes and appeared to be reading something from his mind's eye, something that no one else could see.

"Tradition says that if anyone attempted to take the Flame from the Keeper, they would die. Because even the oral tradition of the Flame has been lost, there is no one who remembers the source of this information. The Torch could only be surrendered upon the death of the Keeper."

Drake just stared at Billy, blinked a few times, and then asked; "Billy, how did you just do that?"

"Do what?"

"You just quoted a book that you don't have in front of you?"

"I just remember things in my mind, and read them off the page. I've always been able to do that, but I never mentioned it to anyone."

"Tests must have been really easy for you?"

"I never used it for school. Once you show people you are smart, everyone expects way too much. It was easier to pass just enough to get through and not be held back."

"You continue to surprise me, Billy Martin." Drake had a smile that could barely be seen in the dim light of the cave.

Billy smiled back because it seemed like a long time since anyone was favorably surprised by him.

After this short break, both of them turned again to see Mr. Furbush, who had already turned ash white from the words Billy had just read from his memory. Furbush knew something new he never realized. He had just come to realize how desperate a situation he found himself in. He was caught between the Torch and the dragons. Not the best known of proverbs, but this was not a book about proverbs, this was really happening to Tunis Furbush. He couldn't give up the Torch because it can't be given up unless the owner dies. And he couldn't meet the demands of the dragons, so he was sure that they would eventually overtake him and kill him, for failing to give them their dragon fire. You don't break promises to dragons! The servitude that the dragons had done was a promise between them and Furbush. It's just that Furbush never knew what his part in the promise was. He was required to give them their flame.

As he sat and thought about what had just been explained, Tunis Furbush sat very quietly. Then slowly tears began to drop from his eyes. Neither Drake nor Billy knew what to say next, so all three sat in a circle while Tunis softly wept for himself and his family.

"There has to be a way out of this. And I have rule number eight - A cowboy doesn't quit."

"This isn't your fight Drake. You and your friends should probably leave before the summer moon is full."

"Cowboys don't quit Mr. Furbush. I don't quit."

"You might wish you had before all this is over. Besides, I thought cowboys had horses!".

Then he turned to Billy and stared for a little while until he finally said, "What about you?"

"Drake's my friend, and if he's staying, I'm staying. It's that simple."

Drake didn't say much. Billy was growing on him and that surprised him. Maybe Jan knew something he didn't about people. He and Billy had some things that needed to be discussed and plans that needed to be made.

Chapter Twenty-Four – The Plan

After Tunis began to walk towards the opening of the cave, Billy and Drake sat down to talk.

"Billy, there is only one way that we can get the Torch from Mr. Furbush. We have to take it from his hands after he is dead. If we can't get that Torch from him, he will be killed by the dragons -- and most likely so will everyone in this town. If the dragons get loose, they will strike with a revenge that hasn't been seen for a long time. I am pretty sure they are already making a plan down in the cave. I can't hear everything they are planning, but they have a side of their character that isn't very pleasant."

Billy laughed, but not very loudly. "That is about the kindest thing you can say about a dragon's character. There are two things that you should know though. Dragons will NEVER break a promise, and they will not lie. At least that is what the books say about them, and they all are pretty consistent about that. "

Drake was deep in thought about that. Perhaps there were some good parts to the most ferocious of beasts. Without looking up, he asked. "Maybe we can use that. Anything else that might help?"

"They really live to collect gold."

"Why do they love gold so much?"

"Never really thought about it. It's part of a dragon's nature. I suppose it has to be the same kind of thing that drives them to desire having the ability to breathe fire."

"What else do you know about dragons that might help us to find a solution to this puzzle? I need to know as much as I can about legends, stories, and rumors that you might have read. There has to be something in the things that you have read that might help us to get the entire town out of danger."

So Billy tried to remember stories that he hadn't already told Drake. They sat there for a while until Billy was running out of things to bring up, and then he noticed Drake looking off to think.

"What's on your mind, Drake? Making a plan?"

"No, not really. Nothing is coming to me. This much I know. The first thing we need to do is to inform the town that they are in serious danger. They must be told they have only two days to get as far away from here as possible."

"Who is going to believe us? We're just a couple of kids from somewhere over the mountain. Kate is the only person who even knows us."

Drake thought for just a moment. "We have to get Mr. Furbush to tell them. He is the only one the people will believe. He has to let people know that their lives and the lives of their families are in danger. If they get a two-day head start on the dragons, some might escape."

"That still doesn't solve the bigger problem – the problem of the Torch."

Drake shook his head. "I got nothing – how about you?"

So Drake and Billy spent the next hour discussing ways to get around the words that were written on the Torch, but nothing seemed possible. There didn't seem to be a way to get the Torch from Tunis Furbush's hands, unless he was dead. There was no way they were willing to do the work of the dragons, by killing Tunis. The only thing they became convinced of was that the people of the town were all in serious danger, and they had to be told. Tunis Furbush had to convince them to leave as quickly as possible. They needed to run for their lives and the lives of those they cared about!

Shortly after agreeing about that, Tunis walked back into the lower cavern, and looked like he was not doing well. The confident walk was gone, and the look of a man waiting on death row was in his eyes and in his shoulders. He mumbled something about dragons and gold, but was generally impossible to understand. He had spent the last few hours thinking about his fate, and the trouble that he had brought on his family and the people of the town. He was already writing his own final moments, as he envisioned being struck down and killed by the largest of the dragons. He had fought one off, but he knew that he could never defend against more than one. Tunis Furbush was not in a good place. Maybe, for just a short time, he had begun to wonder if trying to be rich had cost him too much.

Drake spoke to Mr. Furbush several times before he actually began to hear what Drake was saying.

"Mr. Furbush, can you hear me at all?"

"Oh, yes, of course, I can Drake. What were you saying?"

"You have to tell the people of the town to leave as quickly as possible. I don't know what is going to happen with the dragons, but I do know that they are planning to destroy the town and all that is in it when they take control of the Torch."

"But what about the mine? Who can leave all this behind?"

"All this will bring death on anyone who is still here when the midsummer full moon arrives. Dead people can't spend gold!"

"Yes, of course, you're right. I'll tell them tonight. I'll call a town meeting."

"You have to do it as soon as possible. Close the mine and tell them to meet you in the center of the village."

"Close the mine – but it's only midafternoon. We could still get in a full day's" -- and Tunis stopped himself. "Of course, why continue to mine the gold if we won't survive to spend it. I'll go and call the meeting now, and tell all the workers in the mine to go home."

"It's the only thing to do Mr. Furbush, and it's the right thing to do."

"Yes, of course, it's the right thing to do. Do the right thing, that's what I should do." And without giving it much thought, he looked at the Torch with disgust. Something that he once valued had become undesirable to him. In fact, he was so upset that he considered giving the Torch to the dragons, but Drake had explained to him that it could only be given up if he died, and he wasn't ready to die yet. And as people tend to do when they believe their end is at hand, Tunis Furbush began to believe he could help others before the dragons came for him. It was the first time he had thought of someone else's good before his own for years.

As he quickly rehearsed in his mind what he would say to the people of the town, and how he would explain the situation, he thought that the Torch would be helpful to convince the town's people to run for their lives. He grabbed the Torch and carried it with him as he left the cave. This was the cave within the gold mine that he thought would bring him riches.

Tunis Furbush also knew that if he was attacked by the dragons, the Torch might help him hold them off if only for a little time. Perhaps long enough to save his family, because they did not deserve to die for his poor choices. For the first time in a long time, Tunis Furbush found a small measure of peace that he had not known, because he was thinking about others first. But this peace was hard to recognize since it was so unfamiliar. He had been living without it far too long.

As he walked out of the deep office of the cave, he once again began to step with authority. He had a mission, a task to do, and certainly this would be his most important task. To save his family and the town, all he had to do was tell them about the danger they were in.

As Furbush and the boys climbed out of the mine, at every point Tunis would stop and inform the overseers that the mine was closing for the day, and there was to be a town meeting. At each level, the word spread quickly and many of the workers were climbing out behind Drake, Tunis, and Billy until they finally reached the surface. The sun was completely up, and it wasn't until they exited the mine that Drake and Billy realized that they had been down below since early this morning. The heat of the day was a surprise, not because it was so hot, but the contrast from the coolness of the mine made it feel much warmer than it actually was. Drake remembered that when they entered the mine, the outdoors was cold and the mine seemed warm. Now coming the other direction, the mine was cool but the outside was warm. Something about that temperature difference struck him as odd, and he spoke a comment to himself that he needed to remember that detail. That maybe, somehow, that would play a part in finding a solution -- but he hadn't a clue why. In the past, it had often been something like this that he needed to understand to find the right solution, and this felt like one of those things.

Chapter Twenty-Five – Town Meeting

When Drake and Billy returned to Kate's, both the girls had been concerned about how long they had been gone. Then Drake and Billy begin to explain to them everything that happened in the mine, and their concern quickly turned into fear. Kate wanted her friends to leave now, but Drake and Billy had a different idea. They were going to stay with Tunis Furbush to help him convince the people of the town that they needed to leave Nowhere as quickly as possible.

Word of the town meeting spread as quickly as might be expected in a small village, that really didn't have much news to begin with. No one knew what was going to be discussed, but rumors were really active in the hours before the meeting. Even now people were beginning to migrate to the middle of the town, where the market had been set up just a few days ago. Most of the merchants had packed their carts and moved on, but Jan, Drake, and Billy all noticed at the same time that Pepper McGee's cart was still here. All but Jan had forgotten that they still owed Pepper an explanation, but there was no time for that now. Their apology would have to wait, if it ever came.

As a group led by Tunis Furbush approached the town meeting, the crowd parted to permit him and those with him to proceed to the raised platform. This was where announcements were made in the town center. As Tunis entered the town, he was holding the Torch, and everyone believed it was a weapon. No one suspected the power that lay in the hands of the owner of the Torch, nor the danger that the Torch had for anyone approaching the owner. As word began to spread throughout the crowd that Tunis had arrived, people began hushing each other until the loudest noise in the crowd was everyone telling everyone else to be quiet. When Tunis stepped to the top of the platform, the crowd became totally silent. He then motioned to Drake and Billy to join him on the platform, and the crowd parted for them just as they had for Tunis, not even knowing why these two young boys were so important.

Tunis started his speech just as the sun set in the West, behind the cover of the hills.

"Many of you believe you know the story of how I came to find this Gold Mine, but I have come to you to tell to you the whole story, the part I never explained, and what I have just come to recently understand." Tunis went on to tell them about his quest for gold, finding the dragon who had died of old age, and the discovery of the Torch. He also stated that this was how he was controlling the dragons, but didn't realize why until Drake and Billy showed up and explained why the dragons were serving the owner of the Torch. When Tunis explained this part of the story, the crowd began to murmur until the murmuring grew to anger. There were cries from some that they should steal the Torch and get rid of Tunis, until Drake stepped forward and held up his hands.

"The possession of the Torch can only be taken when the Keeper of the Flame dies. Any effort to take it away from him will kill the person who tries to take possession of the Torch."

One voice louder than the others came from the back of the crowd. "Why are you telling us now?"

Billy stepped up and spoke with surprising authority in his voice. "Because the dragons know that they are only obligated to serve for two years, and the two years is up soon. They will soon be free of their commitment to serve the owner of the Torch."

"Then let them leave – we have plenty of gold already."

Now Drake stepped forward. This was not going like anyone expected it to go. The crowd was getting madder and madder. "Mr. Furbush can't leave, because he can't give them what they expect. When the end of their servitude time comes, they will kill Tunis Furbush and anyone else they can find, once they have taken the Torch. We believe their time of servitude will be finished in two days."

At first, the crowd repeated what Drake had just said. "Two days? Just two days!"

Then it got even louder than before, and grew to shouts as they pressed in tighter and became angrier. Some of the people were angry at Tunis Furbush, but others were angry they were just hearing about this. Some feared for their lives, while others were out for blood. Tunis's blood to be specific, but it didn't look like everyone in the crowd was particular about whose blood. Arms began to fly, and voices rose even more, until it was obvious that someone was going to be hurt. That was when some things began to fly towards the stage. At first, it was only things that were soft like vegetables and such. But then some stones were hurled towards Tunis, and as if by chance, those two stones hit very different marks at almost the same moment. The first stone, the largest, had been thrown by someone far, far back in the crowd, but it was thrown with tremendous force. It landed against the side of Tunis Furbush's head with such force that there was a sickening thud, that once you hear it, it never leaves your memory. The moment Tunis was struck, his eyes rolled back in his head and his knees buckled. The second stone, at almost the same time as the first had found its target. The second one, perhaps by luck, or for those who don't believe in luck, by something stronger than luck, just missed hitting Tunis in the head, but struck the Torch and caused it to fly from Furbush towards Drake. As if by instinct, Drake's hand opened, as he attempted to calm the crowd, and he caught the Torch. The Torch initially burned into his hand, but for some reason, he didn't recoil from the burn, but held on tightly and the burning diminished.

At first, Drake could not believe that he held the Torch. But as he held it, he looked into the writing on the side of the Torch, and was held captive by it. Without translating, he knew what the instructions were, and also just as surely that he would die any moment. But he didn't die. Instead, he was shaken from his shock by the cry of Mrs. Furbush.

"He's dead. You have killed my husband." Mrs. Furbush screamed at the crowd.

When Mrs. Furbush screamed her husband was dead, almost immediately Tamera began to weep as well and ran to join her mother over Tunis. Even though Tamera was at times a very mean girl, she loved her father.

The weeping and screaming of this woman and her daughter made the crowd stop advancing, and a hush fell over everyone there. They all stared at Mrs. Furbush, and listened to her weeping over her husband. She was crying and saying that Tunis was dead, and Drake knew she was right. The only way that Drake could have possession of the Torch was if Tunis Furbush had died. The reason the Torch had burned so much when he first caught it, was because Tunis had not yet died at the moment Drake caught the Torch. The moment the burning from the Torch had begun to diminish was the moment Tunis Furbush had passed from life to death. The feel of the Deepest Mountain Flame still burned, but more like a blister from the heat, than something that was still actively burning into his hand. But still, Drake held tightly to the Torch.

With the crowd silenced, there was, coming from the back of the group, someone who was pushing his way forward to the platform, screaming and yelling at people to get out of the way. It was Pepper McGee who walked forward and grabbed the neck of Tunis. When he first did this, Mrs. Furbush swatted at his hands, but Jan stepped forward and pulled her off Pepper. Jan tried repeatedly to calm down Mrs. Furbush.

"Maybe he can help!"

"He can't help – my husband is dead, you stupid girl. Leave him alone."

"I don't know what I can do, but I have seen Francis do this with animals that had just died and bring them back to life." And with that, Pepper made a fist, lifted it over his head and began to hit Tunis in the chest.

"He's dead – leave him alone."

Mrs. Furbush screamed as she clawed at Jan to let her go. But Pepper continued to pound on Tunis Furbush's chest. Until at last, when Jan could no longer restrain her, Mrs. Furbush got free of Jan's hold and ran to Pepper. She pushed him away from her husband as she cried at the top of her lungs. As she took him in her arms, his eyes blinked twice and then opened. He coughed three or four times, and then appeared dazed, as he looked up at his wife as if to ask "What is all the fuss about?"

For a moment the crowd was very quiet until Mrs. Furbush proclaimed that her husband was alive. And immediately those who wanted Tunis dead only moments ago, were now cheering that he had been brought back to life through the efforts of this traveling merchant. No one really understood how it had happened, and even Pepper who had seen it done to animals wasn't sure why it worked, but it had. That is when Pepper stood to speak to the crowd.

"Your stones and the near-death of Mr. Furbush have not changed this very important fact. In less than two days, the dragons will attack this village, and those who stay here will most likely die. If you want to have any hope of survival, you must flee this place."

"But what about our money? We worked hard in those Mines and we are owed what we earned!"

"I can't tell you about your money. But this I know, dead people can't spend money or gold. If you wish to leave with your lives, you should run away with all you have that cannot be replaced. I suggest you begin with your wives and your children."

As the crowd began to slowly disperse, Mr. and Mrs. Furbush remained on the platform. She was crying, and Tunis was still coming in and out of consciousness. He remained stunned from getting hit so hard in the head.

Drake, however, was staring in silence at the Torch, nearly oblivious to everything that had happened since the Torch had flown into his hand. When he finally did look away, he saw Billy looking at him, and knew that Billy realized what just happened as well. They hadn't killed Tunis Furbush, but the Torch had passed from Tunis Furbush to Drake in those few seconds when Tunis was without a heartbeat.

There was no other explanation. The solution had found them, as is often the case in such things. However, Drake was aware that even when a problem was starting to be solved, other problems soon would pop up. One problem was tied to the burning that he felt in the hand that caught the Torch. It was warm and getting slowly warmer. The Flame of the Torch had entered his body by catching the Torch before Tunis Furbush was completely dead. Drake remembered what Francis had said about the dragon he had tried to help; he only lived three days after the Fire from the Deepest Mountain first entered by touch. Drake hoped he would have three days.

Things had to move forward, and quickly.

Chapter Twenty-Six – After the Meeting

After the crowd slowly went away, those who remained were sure this was some kind of trick to cheat them out of their money. In a short time, there were only a few people who stayed. Drake, Jan, and Billy were not even sure of where to go, but were sure that it would probably be with Kate, since she had stayed behind as well. Mr. Furbush was still not very steady on his feet, and was only just beginning to understand what had happened, as Mrs. Furbush tried to help him back up to his feet. Pepper McGee remained and stared at the three that had left him asleep in his cart, and taken his binoculars without asking. Even before Drake, Billy or Jan offered an explanation he started the conversation.

"I suppose you three will be needing a ride out of town, back to your own homes?"

Jan, who hadn't realized the significance of what Drake was holding began the reply.

"Pepper, we should explain what happened when it seemed like we left you behind and borrowed your stuff."

"That would be nice, but it looks like you three had bigger plans before you ever arrived in this little town."

"We did, but that is no reason not to explain. When we left Francis' home, you were sick, but we refused to leave you behind. We loaded you in the cart and continued down the mountain. When we arrived at a place where we could see the city, we borrowed your binoculars to see where to enter the city. While we were out looking at the city, you woke up and went into town before we could explain. We had planned to come back for you before we entered the town. We must look like horrible people to you."

"In light of all that has happened, I can overlook all that as long as I get my equipment back."

Drake piped up at this, "We need them a little longer."

"But I'm leaving right away. You know about the dragons -- you made the announcement!"

"But things have changed, things have changed a lot," Drake said, both to Pepper, and then turned to look at Billy. Billy was nodding his head.

"A lot, they have changed a lot!" Billy kept repeating and nodding his head.

"I need to talk to Mr. Furbush! I need to ask him about something that happened with one of the dragons." Drake declared.

"He's in no condition to talk to anyone right now. I'm not even sure he remembers his own name, let alone what happened with one of the dragons. You'll have to wait until he's better," stated Mrs. Furbush.

"How long will that take?"

"I don't know," but I do know that he is of no help to anyone right now. I have to get our things together to leave town, and he's not going to be of any help, thanks to someone who tried to kill him with a rock."

"Mrs. Furbush, "They did kill him. He was dead for a moment until Pepper did whatever he did and got his heart beating again," said Drake.

"How do you know that he died, Drake?"

"Because the only way that I can hold this Torch is because it has been passed to me after Tunis Furbush died. It can only be passed on when the owner of the Torch dies, and then can be passed to another."

It was then that Jan noticed that Drake was holding the Torch and her eyes opened even wider as if she was waking up to something unusual. Jan had heard Billy tell the stories, and she was slowly putting all this together. She began to understand that previously, the dragons would have been after Mr. Furbush, but now they will be after Drake. She couldn't see why this was a good thing, which Drake was implying by the glint in his eyes. Kate stood beside Jan, both thinking the same thing. What a bad piece of luck.

Pepper didn't understand the significance of the Torch. Mrs. Furbush knew about the Torch, but saw it as the source of all the trouble presently in her life. She hated this town, and she had wanted to leave since the first day she laid eyes on it. She was not sad about seeing the Torch gone, even if her husband valued it. However even though Mrs. Furbush and Pepper were in the same camp of disliking the Torch, they didn't understand the purpose or the consequences of it. They both wanted to get out of town as much as anyone else, and they wanted to get out as quickly as possible. They wanted to avoid the danger of the pending attack of three very angry dragons.

"Pepper, can we use your cart to take Mr. Furbush home so he can rest while he's getting better?"

"I really need to leave, but I suppose I have time to drop him off there as I'm leaving town. Let me pack up my things and make a space for him."

"Thanks, Pepper!" said Jan.

But Drake and Billy were off to the side of the platform discussing the next part of what they knew they had to do to resolve the problem with the dragons. Billy was also looking at Drake's hand, where the Deepest Mountain Flame had touched him and saw that it was red and swollen.

"If you got the Torch because Mr. Furbush died, why is it burning your hand?"

"I caught the Torch when Furbush was almost dead. I was holding it while he was still alive, so I was burned by the magic of the Torch. But since he died shortly after it was in my hands, I am the owner now. Unfortunately, if the notes at Francis' were right, I have about three days to find a cure to this Flame, or it will consume me from the inside just like it did the dragon."

Billy didn't say a word but looked at Drake's eyes and tilted his head as if to ask the question that wasn't spoken out loud.

"No, I'm not leaving. There is no time. We have to solve this!" Billy had real fear for the first time on this adventure. Billy wondered if the Mountain Flame would kill Drake. Looking at it from a different perspective, Drake knew it was beginning to burn him from within.
Drake knew it would soon kill him if he didn't get some help. Most likely within the next few days, but he couldn't be concerned with that right now. Lives were in danger if he didn't succeed with his plan. There was one question that he couldn't quite resolve – who threw those stones that killed, and then pushed the Torch into his hands. Drake wasn't so young as to believe it was all an accident.

Chapter Twenty-Seven – Preparing for Dragons

No one in Nowhere got much sleep that night, because they were either preparing to move out of town, moving out of town, or already on their way out of town. Not that it matters much if the dragons were intending to find them. One thing about dragons is that despite the presence of burning fire in their bellies, they have a remarkable sense of smell. Some of them do anyway. They can smell gold through solid rock, and they can smell humans for up to 75 miles. If the dragons went looking to kill, there was no cart in town that could take the people of Nowhere far enough away, or fast enough to be safe. Drake knew there was only one solution -- the issue had to be resolved and quickly.

Even before Drake and Billy were back at Kate's house, Billy was asking Drake about his plan. As far as Drake could figure out, he was supposed to be the Master of Ceremonies at an event he had no idea how to run. If it was just a case of giving out merit badges to a group of boy scouts, and he messed up, people might giggle, but in the end, it would all end up just fine. But in the case of dealing with dragons, the stakes were much higher. Without much time to search for more information or become more familiar with the ritual of giving the dragons their flame, Drake had to understand the steps involved and the protections that he would need.

One thing that Drake didn't have time to do was to remember that less than a week ago, he had been hoping to find some kind of adventure. He didn't imagine that it would happen so fast or that there would be so much danger involved. Boredom was where most people live most of the time, and there is a whole lot more safety and comfort in boredom than there is in adventure. And yet, something spoke to Drake deep within telling him that only he could do this thing. Dealing with dragons was not on his list of choices. Drake knew that if he could read their writing, if he could speak their dragon tongue, and if there was no one else in this town that could save the people, then Drake would find a way. He would find a way to keep the people from being at the mercy of angry dragons, and in order to do that, he had to find a way to give the dragons their flame.

Billy was talking to Drake as Drake's mind was working through these things. All of a sudden, it struck him that the key was written on the side of the Torch, which was now in Drake's possession. All he had to do was to read it and understand it. It was only from the writing on the Torch that he could get additional information about giving the dragons their flame.

"Drake, I'm not even sure you have heard a word I have said."

Ignoring what Billy stated, Drake spoke out slowly and deliberately. "The secret has to be in the writings on the Torch. I need to translate these writings, and then we can figure out what to do. There has to be some way we can work this so that no one has to die."

"Speaking of dying, I saw what happened to your hand when you caught the Torch."

Only then did the others in the room see that Drake had been protecting his hand.

"This" he said, lifting up his hand and staring at it. It was only slightly redder now than before. "I think this is the same thing that killed the dragon that Francis noted in his journal. I was only exposed to it for a moment. The amount of time between when I caught the Torch and when Mr. Furbush died. I think the dragon who died at Francis's home had tried to take the Torch from Mr. Furbush while he was still living. I bet Mr. Furbush used it as a weapon. The Torch has some kind of magic in it that makes it stay true to the power that the Creator put into it. Although I wasn't exposed to very much of the Flame, I am sure that any amount will kill you. You cannot take the Torch from the owner as long as he is alive. I hope I have at least three days."

Drake said this all so very matter of factly, that everyone else was concerned. Billy didn't say much because there wasn't much to say. The girls began to focus on Drake's hand, and that wasn't going to help. Drake was determined to stay until one task was done. Drake, Billy, and Jan knew that the only hope for a cure was Francis, who was a few days away, if they left the town now. Drake wasn't going to leave yet. Billy decided not to focus on the elephant in the room, not that there was a real elephant in the room, but Drake was choosing to look to find a solution to the issue of the dragons first. Then Drake had to find a cure to the Deepest Mountain Flame that had begun to burn him from within. This was the only way, and the only order, that the right solution could be found. In two days, the dragons would revolt.

"So let's get planning on this so we can move on from this town. First, let me read you everything on the Torch."

Drake was still as amazed as anyone else that he could read and understand the writing on the Torch. That part of the mystery would have to wait. The immediate concern was that he didn't have anyone to tell him if he was right or wrong, or even just a little right or a little wrong. One other thing that Drake had not noticed was that by having the ability to read DragonSpeak, he didn't realize Billy's change in his willingness to contribute to the group's plan. Billy was beginning to feel that he didn't bring as much value as before, although Drake would not have agreed with that, had he realized what Billy was feeling. But watching Drake read the history of things that were previously unknown, made Billy begin to feel like he was no longer needed. There was a new expert on dragons in the group. This was a feeling that he hadn't felt before the adventure began with Drake and Jan.

While Drake read the writing on the side of the Torch to the others in the room, Kate and Jan took notes in case one of them caught something that the other did not. Billy was quiet in the corner, when Kate looked over and saw the look on his face. She paused, looked over at Jan, who nodded towards Billy, as if to say, "go speak to him." Something was obviously bothering Billy.

"Hey, what are you doing over here?"

"Drake doesn't need me anymore, he's the expert now."

"Just because he can read DragonSpeak, doesn't make him an expert about their history and their nature. You are the only one who knows this stuff. We won't find a solution unless we all work on this. Every time I have ever done anything scary with Drake, he has drilled into me a simple phrase '*we move forward together, we retreat together, and we stay in one place together*'."

"Yeah, he said that to me too, and I'm still here." But Billy still didn't sound like he wanted to stay.

"Billy, listen at me. A person doesn't have to walk out the door to leave. We need you now as much as ever, we need you to stay with us in your head and in your heart. I know that Drake feels that way more than I do."

"You think so?"

All of a sudden, from across the room, Drake slammed something on the table. Hard and loud. "I know so" shouted Drake towards Billy. "I need your help to make a plan on how to use what we know about the promise of the Torch."

A slight smile came across Billy's face and his eyes lit up just a little. Not because he was relieved but because he was needed. Sometimes, being needed is more important than feeling safe or comfortable. At least it is to some people. Billy is one of those people.

"So where are we with getting the information from the Torch?" Billy asked as he walked back across the room and rejoined the group. No one really had a good reason for feeling a little lighter, but they were. Each one of them felt better knowing that everyone was working together to find a solution. There was no other choice.

Chapter Twenty-Eight – A Plan comes Together

After discussing the ins and outs of the process, what the pledge would look like, and how everything should be put into a ceremony, it was Billy who eventually came up with the best solution. The biggest question was, if they could get away with it.

According to what was written on the Torch, it implied that the promises that had to be made by the dragons were firm, but there appeared to be some room to improvise at the discretion of the Holder of the Torch. It was Billy who thought he heard this as Jan read back what she had noted, and Drake had confirmed this by rereading the text on the side of the Torch. It was Drake's idea to deal with each dragon, one at a time, and although the pledge could take more than an hour per dragon, it was the safest way to deal with the larger group of beings that could potentially kill you. Drake also knew that the Code of the Dragons said that they could not lie or break a promise, so he knew once they had pledged, that they would be true to their word. No dragon could resist the desire to be a flame breather. It was that powerful desire that would keep them in control until the end of the process.

The other point that was important to know was that if they broke their promise, the fire would consume them from within quickly. The secret of the flame was in the keeping of the pledge, and if that pledge was broken, the flame would no longer be contained within the second belly of the dragon. Billy had never heard this, because no dragon had ever broken that promise, to his knowledge. Truth is, a few tried and died very quickly, but because the humans had never seen it, it was not recorded in any of the books about dragons.

The passing of the Flame ceremony was as close to a graduation ceremony as a dragon might ever get. They get themselves as clean as dragons can be, and each one steps into the event with a measure of pride. No one but themselves will see what happens, but the dragons held a lot of memories very vividly and would replay this for centuries to come. This event was as close to a sacred ceremony as a dragon would come. It would be the single most important day of their long lives. To mess this up would create hardship that would outlive your children's children to ten generations.

The most distressing part of the ceremony was that Drake was required to walk into the mouth of the dragon with the Torch, and touch it to the back of the throat of the dragon. When this was read from the Torch, everyone turned and looked at Drake, each with a different degree of their eyes wide open.

"You can't be seriously thinking about doing that?"

"The words of the Torch have been true about everything written on it, and I have no reason to believe this is not. I either trust the Torch or I don't. I don't see that I have any other option."

"You know that any one of those dragons could end your life before it's done, and they could even do it by accident."

"A cowboy always keeps his word, and I said I would do what I can. How can we make this as safe as possible? It makes sense to do whatever we can to make this safer."

"If you're really worried about safety, you might want to reconsider walking into the mouth of a dragon."

Drake just smiled weakly and said, "Maybe a helmet of some kind might be useful?"

They all began to look at each other as if someone might be holding back, and then started to laugh at the silliness of it all. Of course, no one thought to bring a helmet with them. So they began to look around the house for some kind of protection from the jaws of the dragon, but found nothing but a cast iron pan which was just too heavy and too clumsy to consider using. Pepper might have something, but he had not been seen since he left the group. Drake thought that he had headed out of town, just like most of the people. Mr. Furbush was one of the few people still in town, because he was too shaken up from almost dying to leave his house. He also knew the simple truth that unless something changed, the dragons would pursue him first of all, and with what little strength he had, he had very little hope of surviving. His only hope was if Drake, Billy, Jan, and Kate could do something and do it soon.

When they found nothing in the house that might help protect Drake's head, while he walked into the mouth of the dragon to light their flames, they decided the best resource would most likely be Tunis Furbush's home. They gathered up everything they needed for the next step, and began the walk towards the Furbush mansion.

Just as they were leaving, Drake stopped in his steps. Everyone stopped behind him not sure what was going on. Was he changing his mind? Was he thinking it might be better to start running now?

"Billy, get one of your books about dragons from the stack and bring it with you. It might be helpful."

"Which one?"

"The thickest one; it doesn't matter. What is the thickest one about?"

Drake had a strong sense of direction and was walking through the town as if he had walked this path 100 times before. He kept up a good pace, not because he was looking forward to meeting with the dragons, but just the opposite, he wanted to get this part over. If he couldn't get his plan to work, Drake feared that he and all his friends might be smoldering ash before tomorrow ended. Nobody looks forward to meeting with dragons who were growing more and more impatient. He tried not to think much farther ahead than that.

While Drake walked ahead of the other three, Billy, Jan and Kate were talking about all the other things that were on the back of their minds, but they didn't want to mention it around Drake.

Jan was the first to say out loud what everyone else was already thinking. "I'm really worried, Drake's hand is not getting any better."

Billy knew the answer but didn't say anything.

"Do you think Mrs. Furbush would have anything that might help? I mean, her husband worked with those dragons for a few years, they must know something," Jan continued.

"There isn't anything that will help stop the burning. The Flame of the Deepest Mountain never stops burning as long as there is something living to burn. If you are touched by the flame, it will continue to burn you until there is no life in you. But this fire burns from the inside out – it is unlike any other flame."

"What can we do for him?" asked Kate.

"The only hope I think he might have is to get to Francis, the healer on Grave Mountain. In his journal, he wrote that he thinks he found the cure for this, but the patient was too close to death to be saved. The dragon who died had waited too long to come to Francis."

"Then we should leave here now. We have to convince Drake to go to Francis right now."

"Wouldn't make any difference now, he's waited too long. We could never get to Francis' house before the Flame overwhelms him. It's too far to travel in the time we have left, and we won't be done with this until tomorrow. The dragons will kill us all if Drake doesn't lead the ceremony to give them their flame, and Drake will die if he takes the time to do it."

Drake looked back over his shoulder and called out to them to let them know he had been thinking about all those details. "I have a plan – keep up with me will ya?"

All three at first were embarrassed that Drake had heard them, but then they all ran after Drake just as he was approaching the Furbush house. Time to see if Furbush owned what Drake needed most to survive the next 24 hours, short of a miracle.

Chapter Twenty-Nine – The Dragons

It was dark outside, but it wasn't stormy – at least on the outside of the cave. But within Ghadhab, there was always a storm of disgust when things did not go his way. Everyone has some of that, but in the heart of this dragon, it was perfected. If there is any beauty in perfect evil, it was found in Ghadhab. He was one of those dragons who believed that everyone had a plot against him. Most dragons felt that way, but Ghadhab was the most proficient at it of these three. He could find evil intentions in any act or gesture, and for that reason, his mistrust of all humanity was growing. It was his stone that had hit Mr. Furbush firmly in the head, and it was his anger that had given him the force needed to succeed in killing Tunis Furbush, if only for a short time. But a dragon's tail, as accurate as it is throwing stones, can only throw one stone at a time. The second stone was thrown by a different dragon.

It was Alghira who was to be feared the most. He could have been voted the dragon most likely to make a plan to get what others have, if dragons were prone to voting. As he had thought about this for the past few months, he had decided that should the opportunity arise, he would take the Torch and get other dragons to submit to him to get their Fire. This is why when he saw Ghadhab throw the first rock, he threw the second one that knocked the Torch out of the hands of Mr. Furbush. He never intended that it should fly into Drake's hand. There was no way that he could have anticipated the quick catch by a human. Most humans are slow, but not tasty. When the time was right, he would attempt to kill the young boy next. Alghira didn't care if human Drake could read and speak DragonSpeak; he had the Flame and Alghira wanted it.

The third dragon in this small group was Hasada. Hasada was more prone to want something without really acting on it, although his own envy for the things of others seemed to have no limit. He also was not a very happy dragon, but happy dragons are things of lore and fairy tales. They don't exist. If you ever think you see a happy dragon, he might be smiling because he just found his next snack. And his next snack would be the one who he is smiling at. Be very careful, because dragons follow their nature, either sooner or later, but eventually they show their true character.

Hasada was the first to speak this morning, just as the dragons were returning to the mine after capturing a few stray animals to satisfy their hunger during the night. I'll not try to write in DragonSpeak their words, because as you know by now, only Drake can read them.

"What horrible bad luck that the boy was able to catch the Torch. Had you waited for just the right time, I could have been the one to catch the Deepest Mountain Torch, and I could be the one to help us get our fire."

"Hasada – you wanted the flame so that you could hold it over our heads, just as Tunis has done for the past two years. We would be no better under your tyranny than his. You want anything and everything that others possess."

"Shut up the both of you. Your useless bickering will not help us get our flame."

"Who made you the leader?" Hasada asked, but not very politely. He was insulted that his own plan had not been considered for even the shortest of moments.

"Do you wish to come against my anger!" called out Ghadhab. "Even without my flame, I am twice the dragon you are, and you know that. I can rip you from wing to tail with just my teeth and claws. You do not want to be the focus of my anger."

Like all living things, dragons have a fear of things that are stronger than themselves. That is generally a good fear. Ghadhab was most decidedly the strongest of the three. He might not have been the most impressive in size, but as the old saying goes, it's not the size of the dragon in the fight, but the size of the fight in the dragon that makes a difference. And the size of the fight in Ghadhab was much larger than any of them, and burned much hotter than theirs as well. None of the other two dragons wanted that anger to focus on them.

Pushing his anger down inside so that he was able to control his thoughts, Ghadhab began to think out loud. "We need a plan to kill this human Drake, and take the

Torch back under the control of dragons. It should never have been in control of humans from the very beginning." The very thought of this mistake since the beginning stirred up the same anger Ghadhab was trying to calm in his own dragon heart. Ignoring his rising heartbeat, he slowly looked up to the others. "We will have to work together again on a new plan."

"Your first plan didn't work out like you said it would."

Ghadhab quickly turned and focused his eyes and anger on Hasada. "Of course it didn't – because Alghira missed the mark. That Torch was meant to land much further away, but he sent it flying into the hands of that boy."

Alghira responded, "That boy should not have been able to catch that. I have no doubt that he caught it before Tunis died. Right now, I am sure the flame is burning him from within."

"It is of no matter to us. We have to make a plan tonight if we have any thought to get that Torch tomorrow. As I just said, we will have to work together."

One of the reasons that dragons were created to be solitary creatures is because situations never improved when they gathered together. Things only got worse. Being together for the last two years had not been easy, but they knew they had to endure this a little longer to get their fire breathing gift from the Keeper of the Torch. Enduring is different than enjoying. But the idea of coming together for a single plan was stretching the limits of their ability to cooperate. Whose plan would they have? Who would be the leader of the plan? Who would be in charge? These were all questions that had to be answered before they could even consider a plan. And this was just too much to do in one night, but they only had one night. One night to come to an agreement about what to do and who should do it. It was going to be a very long night, since dragons can stay awake a long time if necessary, but they didn't like to work that hard. Tonight they would work through the night, and they would be even more difficult to live with tomorrow because of it.

What kind of evil plan can three dragons conceive of to resolve their trouble? One thing was very clear; it was not going to be in the best interests of the Keeper of the Torch of the Deepest Mountain.

Chapter Thirty – Before the Ceremony

Drake never took the time to explain to the others how the Flame was given to the dragons. It was Billy who seemed to understand first, because he began to try to understand the ceremony of the giving of the Flame. It was a graduation type event, but in the place of a diploma, the dragons would receive the ability to breathe fire. The more Billy asked about the details, the more Drake tried to evade the question about how the flame actually got swallowed by the dragons. The one thing that Drake wasn't saying was that he was required to literally walk up to the dragon and step within each dragon's mouth so the flame could be swallowed. If the flame was touched by the sides of the mouth, the dragon would die a painful death. The same death was even now consuming Drake. Once the flame was taken into the dragon's body, for some reason it was no longer dangerous to the dragon, except to force them to keep the pledges they made to the Keeper of the Flame. If at any time in the future they broke that pledge, they would be consumed from within by the Flame.

This, in fact, is the reason dragons were ceasing to be around as much in our days as previously. Very few dragons believed the truth of this pledge, and when they tested that truth, their death was imminent. It was for that reason that Drake determined to read from the Torch to the dragons when the ceremony began. This would not help the dragons live longer, but Drake knew that the survival of his entire group would depend on the dragons believing that the Flame would hold them captive to their pledges. If they were to risk breaking their pledges, they could live long enough to do harm to Drake and his friends, and then they would be consumed by their own fire from within. Their death would be of no help to Drake and company, since the death from the Deep Mountain Flame is slow and painful. There would still be time to cause considerable problems for the people of the town of Nowhere.

Walking away from Furbush's home was the beginning of the long march towards the mine. Drake had to run through a few important points with Billy. Drake had not admitted to his friends the fact that he was dying from the inside out, even though he knew they were discussing that very thing during the walk to the mine. He was determined to carry this weight alone to assure that he could help the others to escape. This was foremost in his mind and although the pain from the internal flame was intense, he would not let it cloud his thinking about helping them to escape.

"Billy, we have to discuss how this will be done. I will have to depend on you to get everyone else away from the Torch Ceremony as soon as it begins."

"But Drake, I wanted to see the ceremony. And you are getting weaker and you might need my help."

"You're right Billy, I am getting weaker. But first of all, I'm the only one who can actually give the dragons their flame. If I don't give them the flame, they'll kill everyone. Even if I do, there is no promise I can control them with the pledges enough to assure they leave us alone. There is even a chance that I will be killed in the process of providing the flame."

"Then let's leave – right now. Why risk death if we might be able to hide from them?"

"Billy, you know that one of these dragons can smell gold through a mountain. What makes you think he can't smell humans from miles away?"

Billy didn't answer for a few steps, and in the silence, he thought he heard Drake stutter in his steps.

"Drake, what's happening to you?"

"The Torch burns the one who takes hold of it before the previous owner dies. I caught the Torch when Furbush was on his last breath, but he was still living. The Flame is consuming me from the inside."

"Maybe Francis can cure you."

"I thought of that, but there is no time to get to him before I am past hope. The best thing I can do is make sure the rest of you can get away. This is why I need you."

"I don't like it, Drake."

"You will need to use the distraction of the ceremony of the Torch to leave the area as fast as you can. Take the rest of our group to the edge of town. I have talked with Pepper McGee, and he will wait for you until noon today. I want to create a long process so that the ceremony will take at least two hours. This will get all of you well out of the city and into the hills. I need that book you brought with you so that I can read from it long enough to stall the final giving of the Flame."

"Dragons aren't known for their patience, Drake!"

"I know, but everyone has more patience when they are waiting for something they really want. I'm depending on their ability to wait for something they want, to be a part of a dragon's character too. I want everyone to help me set up the area as if it were something grand. When I get up and begin to read the book, you are to walk out of view, and then run with everyone to the far side of town. Join Pepper and head up Grave Mountain as fast as you can."

"What if you do survive giving them their Flame?"

"Then I have about 1 day to live with this Flame that is growing inside of me. I would be dead if I ran, and I'll be dead if I stay. Either way, maybe you can save the others."

"Drake? – "but Drake seemed lost in thought.

"Drake, how come just when I think I have found a good friend, I feel like I'm about to lose him? I'm not sure if having friends is worth the cost of losing that friend."

"Billy, I would never have made it this far if you hadn't been with us. I wouldn't even have the smallest portion of my dragon knowledge without your help. I never realized it when you joined us, but you have been and continue to be a very important part of our success, if we do succeed. I may not have much more than a few days, but believe me when I say that I wouldn't trust the lives of Jan and Kate to anyone other than you. You are my friend, whether I'm around to remind you or not."

Billy walked along in silence with Drake for the next short while until the entire group finally reached the opening of the cave that led to the mine, where the three dragons resided.

Drake turned to speak to the group who had joined him and began to tell people their role.

"This is where I need your help. We have to make this a real party. Use everything that we have brought, and what you can find in the cave to decorate. We only have a few hours, but I want this to look as official and special as possible. It is important that the dragons understand the significance of the ceremony because our survival depends on it."

Drake had meant to say "your survival depends on it" because he wasn't sure he personally was going to make it.

No one liked the sound of that, but they had all been warned about this part. As fast as possible the team hung the strings of lights and the shredded paper all around the cave. Lights and torches were brought to lighten up the cave, and within a short amount of time, the place started to take on a festive air. Drake and Billy even found a small stage to set up, that might make the giving of the Flame a little easier on Drake, since the dragons were all so much taller than he was. They could sense that while they were working to decorate the cave, that the dragons hid themselves in the darker parts of the mountain and watched from a distance. Not quite sure of what the humans were doing, but they had never seen this kind of activity in the cave and they, like most dragons, were naturally curious. Of course, they were also suspicious, but that comes with their nature. Where there is no trust, there is no faith in others.

As the hours moved forward, the group used all the decorations they had brought, and everything they had found. There was enough time to sit and talk about how the day would look, and fortunately, Kate had brought along enough food to have a small snack for everyone. Billy was particularly glad to hear this because he had forgotten to eat anything before leaving the house, and the fact that he was very hungry was catching up to him.

Jan was the first to ask. "So, what is the plan for the ceremony?"

Billy had his mouth full, and just mumbled something, and then tilted his head towards Drake as if to say – ask him. Kate did look up and stare from Drake to Billy and then back to Drake with the same question in her eyes, but without voicing it.

Drake took a deep breath; more and more that was the kind he took since he was not feeling at full strength.

"We will call the dragons into this portion of the cave, and I will direct them where to sit. I will stand on the stage that Billy and I found, and then you should all be behind me. I have asked Billy to bring one of his larger books, and I will read from it in order to give a little more time to the ceremony. When I begin reading, you are to silently, one by one, leave the cave. The purpose of reading is to give all of you time to sneak out of the cave, and join Pepper who will be waiting for you on the far side of town."

"And that's where we wait for you to join us?"

Drake just looked up and shook his head. "I have made other plans."

"And we are supposed to leave you alone with the dragons! That is not going to happen."

"Kate, it has to happen this way. I cannot be sure of your safety unless you find a way to be as far as possible from the dragons and me. I need you here for the beginning of the ceremony. Your presence will add to the importance of the ceremony. I need you to be the audience, and having an audience should help the dragons to comprehend the importance of it all. Imagine you are watching someone get their diploma."

"Yeah right. Their graduation to have the ability to cook us all alive!"

"Your presence is critical to helping me survive this, if I am going to survive."

"But how will you get away?"

"I have a plan, but I'll have to play this by ear."

There was a lot of silence, at least it seemed that way, until Jan spoke up. She didn't agree with leaving without Drake. She knew it was sarcastic before she said it, but it came out anyway. "Well, you still have two ears; let's hope you don't lose em."

Chapter Thirty-One – The DragonTorch Ceremony

When noon arrived, everyone knew it was the hour. The reason is that the Torch is at the zenith of its strength, when the sun is at its highest and is the closest to the earth. That was this day and this time. Drake knew there was nothing left to do but get started. Yet he really didn't want to get started. He turned and looked at his friends, and realized that he might not ever see them again, but he had to stop himself from thinking that. Drake stood up from the bench, made of stones from the quarry, that he had been resting on and slowly walked to the middle of the platform. It was not very large, but it lifted Drake up a little and gave him that extra air of importance that was needed.

As he walked, he looked around at the newly decorated cave, and thought how hard everyone had worked to add some life to this dark place, but it was still a cave. The dark rock walls were still the most obvious part of the room, and the dirt and rock floor was still dirt and rock. But there was more color and light than this small cavern had ever seen before. As Drake stepped on the platform, he was just a bit melancholy about his friends. He would miss them, and if he ever got to see them again, he would make sure that he told them how much he treasured each one. But now was not the time to make that declaration. But if not now, when would he have the time or the opportunity? As he arrived on the wooden platform, he stepped to the middle and turned towards them before doing anything else. He had to say something.

"Friends, we have been through some difficult things and travels together. There are no words grand enough to express my appreciation for your help in all we have done, and the people we have rescued in this town. Whatever happens today, you are as fine and remarkable a gift as any I have ever had."

Then Drake turned to the cave and called out the dragons one by one, name by name.

"Alghira, come forth. Hasada come forth. Ghadhab, come forth."

Most of the others didn't understand what Drake was saying because Drake was calling out in DragonSpeak, although Billy thought he did catch some of what was said. He didn't get the names, but understood the dragons were being called up one by one. Drake and his friends waited for them to arrive, but for some reason, they didn't arrive even though they were not that far away. Billy thought he could hear them breathing, but Drake knew they were standing just outside of the light in the main cavern. Drake called them out again.

"Alghira, come forth. Hasada come forth. Ghadhab, come forth."

And still, there was no sound of anything stepping towards the light. Drake began to doubt his own ability to use DragonSpeak, but then it occurred to him that perhaps he could coax them out. He turned to the group and then shouted the thought.

"I think if you sing something, they'll come out. "

Everyone just looked at Drake like he had just asked them to put their shoes on their ears.

Kate was, as usual, the first to question this.

"What do you expect us to sing?"

"It doesn't matter, just sing something loudly!"

Kate turned to the group and asked, "Is there a song we all know?"

After a few moments, no one came up with anything, so Drake turned and waved his hands at them to go ahead and start singing. Jan started up first, and then the others joined in singing with all they had within them.

"Happy Birthday to you, Happy Birthday to you, Happy Birthday, Happy Birthday, Happy Birthday to you."

Drake smiled at the weirdness of it all, and turned to tell them to sing it louder and repeat, until he asked them to stop.

So the chorus began again, this time with more volume and more exuberance.

In case you did not know, dragons are not used to singing. Most of the time when they hear human voices, it is not singing but screaming. This singing was most curious to them, and they slowly walked in from the darkness they were using to conceal themselves. As they walked into the larger cavern, the chorus slowly faded until only Billy was singing, and between you and me, he was the worst singer in the group, maybe in the whole town. He sounded even worse with his mouth barely able to close as the three dragons came into view. It might have been funny if it weren't for three very large dragons standing before the team.

The cavern became brighter when the dragons entered because of the reflective nature of their scales, and it was that same reflective nature that makes the colors hard to explain. There were all the colors of the rainbow and then some. If you have ever seen the sunburst over the mountains in the early morning of spring, you might have seen some of the colors that came from the dragons. It wasn't clear if some of the range of colors would have been different in natural light, but there were all the primary colors, almost as if each dragon scale had been hand-painted by impressionist artists. When you are too close to impressionist art, all you see are the small dots that the artist uses to create a larger masterpiece. But when you stepped back, you saw the art as a whole, as the artist expected you to see it. So that the individual colors were beautiful, and if you were able to take your eyes off the individual scales and step back, you begin to notice the theme in each dragon's outer protection. Few eyes on earth had ever seen these colors, and fewer still that lived after seeing them. Their beauty was greater than anything anyone would have imagined. But for all their beauty, no dragon's beauty could take away the truth that they are dragons, and they are still very dangerous. The more beautiful, the more dangerous, was what Billy had explained. Drake looked at them and tried to size them up, to see who would be the last to go through the Ceremony of the Torch. Most of the rest of the conversation is in DragonSpeak, but that is of no use to those who will read this story, so I'll put it in normal English.

"Dragons, declare your names to me!"

Billy turned from watching the dragons and stared at Drake. In just moments, Drake had gone from being sick to being full of more strength than Billy had ever seen in him. It was as if Drake knew that he must convey power to these dragons or be consumed by them. And Drake also knew that if he was consumed by them, his friends would also be taken. Drake's determination for the task exceeded his natural strength, but that's true about all heroes. They find their strength at the moment it is needed the most.

The largest one stepped forward – "My name is **Hasada**, who addresses the dragons?"

"My name is Drake, Keeper of the Torch of the Deepest Mountain Flame, speaker of the language of dragons, and you are held by your pledge to the Torch to obey me." As he said these words, he held the Torch of the Deepest Mountain Flame high above his head, and it seemed as if for a moment, the flame that had already begun to consume Drake wasn't going to weaken him. But carefully, Drake was aware not to spend too much strength holding the flame above his head.

The smallest one stepped forward next, "My name is **Ghadhab,** renown for my anger and temper. We have served the Keeper of the Torch these two years as pledged. We will **not** serve a New Keeper for two more years."

Drake noticed there was fire in this one's eyes, and he hadn't yet received his flame. "Your time of service is complete. I am here to finish the task of imparting the Deepest Mountain Flame."

This news took all the dragons by surprise, since they were sure that the humans would try to cheat them out of what they had earned by their service. In fact, it brought Alghira from his concealment even though it had been planned that he would remain hidden by the darkness. "My name is **Alghira**, known for my desire for other's things. It is my desire to have a part of all that I can get."

Both Hasada and Ghadhab looked at Alghira in disgust, knowing they could be the target for his desire.

As is so often the case, few plans can succeed if they go against the true nature of those who participate. Alghira would not stay back if he thought he was missing out on anything. But for the time being, this appeared to be going better than anyone of the dragons had thought that it would go.

"Who among you should have the honor of being the final dragon in this Ceremony?"

This was new to the dragons, that there could be any honor in being last. It went against everything in their nature to desire to be last, for each one of them down to their very core, wanted to be first. And yet, each one wanted to be in a role of honor. Since Drake seemed to know what to do, and had the air of someone in charge, each dragon stepped forward at the same time, causing the cavern to shake with their combined weight. But not one of them could restrain their feet from wanting to have any and all honor possible. Drake had counted on this.

"Good, all of you understand the honor it is to be the final dragon awarded your flame. This is proof to me that you understand the importance of being last.

Drake spoke to the dragons with great authority, but if you knew him well, he looked tired. "Now this is not a ceremony for these others to watch, for they have not earned the right to observe. I will dismiss them now, for we have no need of them."

Kate was the first one to refuse to leave, then the others broke in and promised they would not leave without Drake. Drake put his hand up to the dragons, as if to have them wait, and walked slowly over to his small band of friends.

Then in a whispered voice, he pleaded with his friends. "I have a plan to get us all back home, but you must leave now and meet me at Francis' home, on the mountain. But if you all stay with me, I fear it could cost all of us our lives. I don't have time to discuss this, only to ask you to trust me."

Jan spoke out – "How will you get there, you are still being consumed by the Deepest Mountain Flame?"

"There is no time to discuss this. Leave now and go to Francis' home. I will meet you there. I need you to leave now!"

All of Drake's friends were shocked! Most of all Billy, who had just recently begun to embrace the truth that you never leave anyone behind. Drake must have seen this in his eyes because he turned to Billy and walked him aside. Then Drake told Billy something that took Billy by surprise.

"Billy, you have grown to be my friend. I didn't want to bring you on this trip, and now I know that I could not have made it to this point without you. Now, I must trust you to get everyone up to Francis' home as quickly as possible and keep them safe. I know I have told you never to leave someone behind, but this is that exception. And you have to convince them to hurry out of town quickly and get into the hills."

"Drake, you're the first real friend I've ever had. I didn't think I needed friends, and now I do. I can't leave you with those dragons."

"Billy, if the dragons turn on me, you could not do anything to stop them or slow them down. And I need to know that everyone will be safe so that I am free to do what must be done. If you take everyone up the hill, that is the greatest help you can be to me."

"I don't like it, but I'll do it. If you aren't at Francis' house, I'm coming back to find you."

"Thanks, Billy, I'm in your debt for your help."

Billy returned to the group and began to walk them towards the opening of the cave. And though they all protested, Drake knew that Billy would take charge, and they would do what he asked them to do. Drake took a deep breath and prepared to meet the dragons -- and stall as much as possible. In this action of giving them their fire, he was hopeful that he could get out of this with his own life. He was working against four things, three of them were very large dragons, and the fourth was the ever-increasing internal burning that he knew to be the fire from the Deepest Mountain flame. It was slowly consuming him from the inside out.

Chapter Thirty-Two – The Stall

Drake didn't have an exact picture in his mind of how things would progress, but he knew he had to stall long enough to let his friends get out of town and into the mountains for their own protection. He also knew that he had to figure out which dragon might be the most inclined to keep a promise. So he quickly tried to come up with questions that would test the character of these dragons.

"I must determine who shall get the honor of being last. There is no record of three dragons getting their flame at the same time, so this must be done correctly and with the honor that is due."

All three of the dragons stepped forward and looked at Drake with a new curiosity because he sounded so confident. None of them even thought that he was making everything up, but he was. Drake had no record of any dragon ever getting their flame, let alone three at the same time.

So he stepped forward, and with a loud and authoritative voice asked the smallest dragon, **Ghadhab**, "How would you describe your fellow dragons?"

The other two, who were standing on each side of Ghadhab, took a step back and turned from watching Drake, and began starring at Ghadhab, curious what he might say.

"My brothers both desire anything they can imagine, and will never find satisfaction."

Drake was taken back and was afraid that Ghadhab had insulted the other two. Strangely, both the other dragons appeared pleased with Ghadhab's description of them, even if their smiles were more frightful than their snarls. Drake listened and thought and stalled.

"Ghadhab, you have spoken wisely. For that is what their names tell me they are. **Hasada** tell me about your brothers."

Hasada didn't answer the question, but insisted on being asked last. Drake had to explain that this was to determine who will have the honor of being last, so Hasada spoke.

"My brothers are very different. One seeks what another has, but would never risk a battle. The smaller one has a depth of anger none of us have ever dared to face, nor tried to measure."

Drake was still trying to measure what had been shared, when the third dragon stepped forward to speak.

"We are growing weary of your games, human. Give us the Flame or I will sacrifice my own life to take your life. We slaved for the human Furbush for two years, longer than other dragons before us, and we will not slave another day. Give us our dragon fire or we take our vengeance out on your kind first, and then return for you. "

Drake turned slowly towards Alghira, "I know that you desire more than others to have this Flame, and that you would willingly send any one of your brothers to their death that you might have what you have earned. I promise that each one of you will get your Flame today. But I must have two promises from each of you before I give you your Flame. And for repayment for your promises, you may divide the remaining gold among yourselves. I have no need of your gold."

When Drake said this, each of the dragons took such a deep breath that it felt as though all the air from the cave was suddenly gone. They collectively looked at Drake, and then at each other, because their perception of gold was that everyone wanted all they could have or carry. Their understanding of all mankind had been understandably twisted by working for Tunis Furbush, but they thought it was true none the less. They thought all humans were the same.

The dragons turned and discussed among themselves softly so that Drake could not discern what they were discussing. There was considerable wagging of the head, both affirming and then negating their compliance. Finally, after about five minutes, with a little bit of heated arguing, they turned as one to Drake.

Alghira spoke out. "We must hear the promises before we agree they will be kept."

Drake already knew what the promises would be, but stalled. He knew that every moment that the others were able to get away from the town increased the likelihood that if this went bad, they might at least save themselves. So, placing his hands behind his back, Drake walked up and down before the dragons, moving ever closer, holding the Torch above his head as much as he was able. His weakness was getting greater and he could feel it, but he resisted allowing the dragons to sense he was slowly dying from the Torch's flame.

The First promise is this: You shall not harm, hurt or eat any humans.

This was the part that Drake feared the most. Each dragon responded in their own way, but for the first few minutes, there was only silence. They had never heard of a dragon who was not allowed to harm, hurt or eat humans. There is no history of dragons and humans living together. This went against all dragon lore and history. How could he ask such a thing, so they went into their own counsel again, three large dragons. This time, they were each more agitated than before. Drake could not make out much, but he smiled softly when he heard Ghadhab say loud enough to be heard, that humans really didn't taste that good anyway. Evidently, Ghadhab preferred sheep and horses.

Alghira said: "But this promise shall remain in place only as long as the humans don't attempt to harm dragons."

Drake understood that, and so he answered: "Of course"

But then they turned quickly and stared at Drake, and almost in unison said: That's three promises!

Drake quickly responded. "No, it is only one."

Hasada stepped forward and the cave shook with each step. "That is the first promise, what is the second?"

Drake took a breath and pushed his body to be as tall as possible. I shall ask from one of you, the transportation to Francis the Healer when we have finished. He lives on the far side of the mountain. I have something I need to discuss with him. The one who takes me there shall be free of all future promises. The others will be in my debt for a future time, as such I may need. I may never ask for your help, but you must be willing to help if called."

The dragons once again retreated into a circle where they discussed if they were willing to obey the conditions. There was a lot of yelling, but that is how dragons dispute. They don't simply express their opinion, and even if they agree, they still yell at each other. This is one of the many reasons they live alone. They are like some people who appear mean to outsiders, when the truth is, they are mean to each other too. Some countries had people like that too. It seemed like this was taking more time than it should but whenever there are three dragons together, which is extremely rare, there are five different opinions. They were not made to be social to anyone or anything, even other dragons. Finally, after all the discussion was talked out, the question was asked how much gold was there? This seemed to snap them back to agreement, and they turned to Drake and said all at the same time:

"We are willing. We will keep the promises!"

Chapter Thirty-Three – The Flame Delivered

It was a good thing that most of the directions about how to light a dragon's flame were on the Torch, although Drake was concerned that he would have to touch the Torch to the back of the tongue of each dragon. It came to Drake's mind from nowhere that the dragons should extend their tongues as far as possible so that he didn't have to enter their mouths as deeply to light their dragon fires. Drake spoke some words and he honestly didn't remember what they were. He knew that none of them had ever seen the event, so he also knew that they had no idea about how it should go. But Drake had read about how knights were christened and decided that seemed like a reasonable picture of what was happening here.

Making sure there was some delay was also important to Drake since he knew that every minute the dragons were delayed, was one minute more that all the people of the town had to escape possible destruction. The other problem was that Drake was actually getting weaker every minute too, because of the effects of catching the Torch moments before Furbush was temporarily dead. If he went too long without getting treatment from Francis, Drake knew he would die, and the Torch would pass to the next person who picked it up. That was the hardest thing to imagine. The more time he could delay, the more time his friends could have to escape, and the closer he would come to dying.

One thing that Drake decided to change seemed important to him. Drake had always thought that everyone adopted the characteristics of their name. So in thinking about the names of the dragons, Drake imagined that if he knighted them with new names, maybe over the years, they might grow and change into their new names. Drake renamed Hasada to be Rashaqa, in the hopes that he would learn to give more than desire. He renamed Ghadhab to Yahtawaa, in the hope that his anger would soften. He renamed Alghira to Maet, thinking this might help him overcome his jealous nature.

Each one was dismissive of their new names, but shortly after each had their flame, Drake began to address them by their new names. The selection of which dragon would fly him to Francis's home was not an easy one. One of the dragons was already becoming Drake's favorite, if you can have a favorite dragon. But the one he chose to fly him to Francis' house would be the one he would most likely never see again. Putting all that aside, he stepped forward and spoke to the dragons.

"It should take you about 7 days to empty the gold from the caves below. I suggest you wait until tomorrow to divide the gold, since you have your fire now. Each of you can melt down what he can carry, and store it away to be taken back to your home. Today, I will need the services of Maet to fly me to Francis' home. After you leave me there, you will be free of your second promise, although I will hope our paths will cross again somewhere in the future. I must leave soon for Francis needs my help and I cannot stay any longer with you. Maet, please dismiss yourself from the others. And both of you, wait until Maet returns to begin dividing up your gold."

"Rashaqa and Yahtawaa both owe me their promise, which I shall reserve for future use. I will promise this to both of you. The fulfillment of your promise will not involve giving me any of your gold. You have earned that."

Then for good measure, not sure if it was important, Drake said, "Now that you all have flame, you must respect the Dragon's Code."

And so it happened that Drake was able to ensure that the dragons kept the code that was written on the base of the Torch. "I will not hold slaves, I will not kill for the joy of killing, I will not band with other dragons to rule the earth."

Drake didn't actually know for sure if this was the Dragon's Code, but evidently all the dragons thought it was, and agreed to maintain it. He thought perhaps to ask more about the Dragon's Code, and what that code was, but fatigue was beginning to overwhelm him more than curiosity. So he turned to walk out of the cave. As he did so, he suddenly realized how weak he was. He stumbled slightly and all the dragons watched to see if perhaps something was wrong. Instead of admitting it, he called to Maet, slowly climbed upon his back, and ordered him to take him to Francis' house, on the far side of the mountain. Oddly, it seemed that every animal, even dragons, knew about Francis.

One thing that Drake had not expected was that dragons typically fly much higher than one would expect. As he held onto Maet with one hand, the other clung tightly to the Torch even though his strength was leaving him. The higher Maet flew the more light-headed Drake became. As Maet rose higher, Drake remembered that he didn't like heights, so he firmly closed his eyes. Just before he closed his eyes, both from weakness and fatigue, his thoughts were, "whatever happens, don't let go of the Torch." As he drifted off, his last thought went to his friends, whom he hoped to see again. Drake had not realized how very close to death he was, and he had no way of knowing if his actions had saved the lives of anyone. He had only hoped that by trying, he gave them at least a chance of survival. In fact, his actions had indeed saved his friends and everyone in the town. But he wouldn't know that for sure for a few days.

But for now, Drake fell asleep repeating to himself "Don't let go, don't let go, don't let-." Drake drifted off to sleep saying those words to himself with the hope he would not let go of the dragon or the Torch.

Chapter Thirty-Four – Waking Up

When Drake finally did wake up again, he felt like he was being bounced around. It took some time, since he was so groggy, but soon realized he was in the back of a cart. He actually didn't really know where he was because he was covered in blankets, and the gentle swaying of the cart caused him to drift in and out of sleep a few times, before his thirst forced him to sit up and look for something to drink. It was only then that he heard the voices of Jan, Billy, and Pepper and he came to grips with the fact that he was alive, and that he was laying down in the back of Pepper's cart.

"Can I have something to drink?" asked Drake, interrupting their conversation.

"Hey, Drake is awake!" called out Billy with a loud cry, and the rest of them turned and started laughing and talking even more.

Pepper stopped the cart quickly, and they all jumped down and walked around to the back of the cart. Jan was hugging Drake, Billy was shaking his hand, and Pepper was patting him on the head like some kind of little puppy. Drake tried to hug back but he was too weak to do that.

"You're awake – how are you, how you feeling?" "You've been sleeping for days, it was touch and go for a while there." These were phrases that the three of them were saying, but Drake could not be sure who was saying what. He was still a little drowsy and dizzy from sitting up. He wasn't sure what question to answer first, or what questions he had about what they had just told him.

"Can I please have something to drink?" asked Drake again.

"Of course – sit still, don't move too much. You have been asleep for about three days."

Drake didn't really care who said that, but it was Jan.

"Three days?" He looked right to Jan, as he slowly drank from the canteen that Billy handed him. His words, though few, wanted the whole story.

"We don't know everything, but one of the dragons brought you to Francis' house before we got there. Somehow he convinced Francis to take you in, and treat your injuries from the Deepest Mountain Flame that was killing you. Even though Francis has no concern for humans, because he thought your case interesting, he agreed to take you in and try to cure you. He had learned enough from the first dragon that had died that he thought he could heal you and he did. However, as soon as you were healed, he was looking to move you out of his house. That's when we arrived at his house, two days after you did."

"As we approached the house, Francis met us at the edge of his land and warned us that we could not stay with him, and that one of our party had been dropped off by a dragon. We knew it had to be you. He didn't remember your name. But he said you came in very sick, and now you were better, and that you were smelling up his house with the smell of humans, and we needed to take you off his hands. We tried to pay him for his care, but I guess Francis doesn't need money because he refused to take any from us. We loaded you in Pepper's cart, and we have been heading home since we got you, which was about one day ago. We are almost down to Billy's fort, where we first met Pepper."

While Drake slowly drank water and nibbled from the available food scraps, Billy, Jan and Pepper filled him in on everything that happened in the town, and with the people. Everyone had survived and run away before the dragons ever came out of the caves -- except for the one dragon that flew out of the cave, and took you to Francis' home.

"What happened to the Torch," Drake asked, not sure if it had survived the journey, but also fearful that should anyone else try to use it, it would kill them if Drake were still living.

It was Billy's turn to fill in the details. "Francis asked about that and I explained what it was and how it was cursed. If anyone tried to use it, it would take their life. He agreed to keep it for you, and you can get it when and if you need it.

Francis seems to be the kind of person who doesn't have a love for money, so I thought it would be safe with him until needed."

"Billy, I --." Drake wanted to tell him again how he never realized how much he was needed. Drake was surprised at the feelings that were welling up within him in appreciation.

Billy just nodded and stopped Drake from saying it again. "I know".

Billy wasn't really prone to crying, but Jan could make up for what he lacked. Still his eyes were moist. And Pepper, just sat there looking forward so no one was sure what he was thinking. Just as well, since the day was getting late and Drake's home-town was just over the next hill. They were already seeing signs of people and outlying houses in the distance. But before the opportunity passed, Drake turned to Pepper, caught his eyes, and mouthed one simple word – "Thanks." That was all that Pepper needed to know -- he was appreciated too.

About that time, Drake pulled the blanket back over his head and closed his eyes. He began to think about their remarkable adventure. As he reviewed the events in his head, he remembered that he needed to get over and mow Mr. Winter's lawn because he said he would.

And for Drake, that was as good as a promise.

THE END

END NOTES:

Drake is in remembrance of my younger brother, Larry Drake Allen, who died much younger than he should have. Larry had a kind heart and mind that slipped back and forth because of being bi-polar. When it was really him, he was as kind as a person could be. This Drake however doesn't have much in common with Larry except his name.

Mr. Winters – my Dad looked a little like Johnathan Winters. No actually he looked a lot like Mr. Winters. I slept in a room with my two older brothers and Dad used to read us jokes from a joke book when we got into bed at night. He even would make the faces and do the voices of the people in the joke. My brothers and I would turn out the light laughing and repeating the punch line into the darkness of the night. It is a great memory.

Billy Martin was the neighborhood bad kid. Doesn't hurt that his name is also one of the better known baseball coaches in history. This Billy gave me my first firecracker which nearly blew up in my hand. I still have all my fingers, but it was close. In this story, I plan to reform Billy, something I don't believe ever happened to the real Billy.

This is also a nod to my grandson, Jonathan, who when we were all gathered around, we heard a loud noise from his room, and then this small voice called out to assure us that he was "all right". That happens when Drake falls from the tree.

I chose Pepper's name and mixed it with his brother's name for two reasons. The Pepper I knew was always ready to help and I like that name for a character in the book. I like Pepper and he doesn't get the explanation that he deserves as to why the kids left him and the cart until later.

Francis was named after the patron saint of animals. He is a healer and prefers animals to humans.

Tunis Furbush This is a combination of the names of two prominent carpetbaggers in the post-civil war reconstruction, one named Tunis Campbell and the other named William Hines Furbush. Carpetbaggers were not nice people. Look them to know what they did.

Translation on the side of the DragonTorch

I will not	Hold	slaves			
Drakona s ka	Sakra	petim a			
I will not	Kill	For	The	Joy	Of killing
Drakena s ka	putros	ő	Dak	Falam a	putroso s
I will not	Band	With	Other dragons	To rule	The earth
Drakena s ka	garento s	æõ	Drakeno s	domu s	Terros

A literal translation is

Death to	The One	Takes from	The ruler	The Torch Keeper
Putrosa	Onomas	Volarat	Domus	Logi-Markvörður

Rashaqa	graciousness
Yahtawaa	content
Maet	Giver

Post reading notes:

I wanted to add a few notes about the messages I wrote into the story that might not have seemed obvious at a casual read. However, I feel inclined to point them out in case they were missed. First, it is the lesson of living by a higher purpose. Drake is driven by his code, and you will see a few times that he refuses to leave Billy behind, even before he begins to like Billy. I know that everyone needs to have a higher calling, and each of us must find what that calling is. One of the things Drake has is a very deep sense of loyalty towards those he promises his word. You might even have noticed that at the very end of this book, he is reminded that he had promised Mr. Winters that he would mow his lawn. After saving a town, this is what comes to mind. Keeping his word. A person will be highly respected if they keep their word. That alone is worth remembering.

The next thing that seems important to point out is the relationship between Drake and Jan. They were friends who were of the opposite sex, but they were not romantically involved. At the imagined age of our two main characters, that is not a surprise, but my point is to show that not every male and female, who are together in a story, have to have a romantic relationship. They are different than each other but it is the strength of their differences that makes their relationship or teamwork so productive. I tried to point that out in the way that Jan viewed Billy. Jan was willing to give Billy a chance because he was needed. Drake did not and Drake was wrong. Heroes are sometimes wrong, which might have been the biggest surprise to Drake throughout the entire story. Then he thought he knew about Billy, but he did not. And in fact, it is one of the strengths of Drake that he discovers he was wrong and admits it to Billy.

Another thing that is of great interest to me is the slow restorative power of someone who feels as though they are a valuable part of a team. Billy had a home life that is terrible but that didn't make him a terrible person. It did make him meaner before the story begins, but his worth was not defined by the home he grew up in. In fact, he was so accustomed to failing that he preferred failing to showing that he was smart. We all measure intelligence in several ways, and I have been mistaken when I didn't try to look below the surface and find hidden talent within every person. I hope you don't look at people like Billy, and think just because they act one way, that they have little worth. All people have great value that is often waiting to be discovered by another person who believes in those who come from a less supportive background than their own.

www.ingramcontent.com/pod-product-compliance
Lightning Source LLC
Chambersburg PA
CBHW060139130626
46556CB00006B/2412